The
Starlight
Lancer

Other works by this author:

Final Flight of the Ranegr
The Awakening
Path of a Hero
The Cursed Jewel
Metanoia
The Star Warriors

Find them online at
https://www.cscooper.com.au/books

The Starlight Lancer

C. S. Cooper

For my Mum and Dad, who supported me and convinced me to publish this series.

CONTENTS

Acknowledgements

I acknowledge Nobuhiro Watsuki, whose manga inspired this story. I also thank the people who read my novel, *Final Flight of the Ranegr.* Since you were so intrigued by *The AXOM Saga,* and requested paperback copies, here you go. Then, there are my parents and family, who encouraged me to publish it.

1 | Just a nightmare

There are plenty of rules for conduct within the campus of Warrawul Boarding School, as with any school in Wollongong – or anywhere else for that matter. The first one that comes to mind is 'Show up for class on time.' Mr. Chamberlain had become particularly strict about that in recent days. If you were but a second too late, instant detention for you! In a biopic of Ol' Chambo's life, the guy who played Voldemort would score the lead role.

There are also the rules that aren't written in the school charter: those exist in the minds of the boarders who occupy the dormitories just down the road where the Princes Motorway connects to the Princes Highway. Those unspoken rules, diversified between the girl's and the boy's sides of the building, include hanging something on the doorknob if you're entertaining your boyfriend or girlfriend – for the girls, it's a hat; for the boys, a sock (and if you switch them around … well, it's one way to come out of the closet).

The most well known and sacred of the dorm rules is 'Obey the curfew.' If you don't, the manager will report you to the school the next morning. And you'd best pray Ol' Chambo doesn't find out.

Nathan disobeyed that rule one night, during the first week of the first term of the year. He'd only been back at school for a week, and already had a tonne of homework. Despite his earnest efforts to get it done as quickly – and as half-arsed – as possible, he had taken far too long on this particular night. And he knew if he didn't get his nightly workout done, he'd go nuts the next day. So he skipped dinner, and headed straight for the dormitory gym.

Ten sets of ten push-ups! Ten sets of ten sit-ups! Ten sets of ten chin-ups! Bench-presses! Bicep curls! Squats!

Nathan had long since surpassed his best friend and fellow gym-bro, Klein, who that night watched him with admiration and a twinge of alarm.

"Done!" exclaimed Nathan, finishing his post-workout stretches. "Now, for some cardio!"

All the treadmills and cross-trainers were taken.

"Too bad," said Klein with a smirk. "You'll have to call it a night."

"No way, man!" retorted Nathan with a grin. "I'll just go out."

"It's past curfew," said Klein as he followed Nathan out of the room.

"It's alright, the manager likes me," replied Nathan.

Klein rolled his eyes. "No he doesn't! Remember when you ate all that vindaloo and blocked the toilets?"

"That was you!" retorted Nathan as he strode down the dormitory corridor toward the exit.

"No, *you* spent almost half an hour on that toilet," replied Klein with an accusatory point of his finger. "*I* was done in five minutes. *You* had to have seconds of that curry."

"Yeah, 'cause I work out all the time," chuckled Nathan.

"Too much of the time," replied Klein, a twinge of worry to his voice. "You shouldn't over-exert yourself, man. You're gonna get hurt one day."

Nathan stopped and swivelled to look at his friend.

"Dude, I'm fine," he said, his breathing slightly hitched. "I'll just run to the *Chickos* and be back." Klein shot him an annoyed glare. Nathan replied with a reassuring pat on the shoulder. "I appreciate you're lookin' out for me, man."

Klein returned a smile. The mood went quiet and tense as the two boys locked eyes. Klein stepped closer, as did Nathan. Their lips gravitated toward each other. Nathan suddenly pulled back and growled, "Goddamn it!"

Klein punched the air with both fists and yelled triumphantly, "Oh, yeah! I am still king of gay chicken!"

With faux anger, Nathan caught his friend in a headlock and snarled, "You should play against someone who's actually gay."

"I have, and I still won," retorted Klein cockily.

"How?" bellowed Nathan.

"Didn't brush my teeth for three days," grunted Klein, struggling against the headlock.

Nathan thought a moment, before releasing Klein and humming with approval.

"Yeah, that'd work," he said. "Impressive, man."

"Not nearly as impressive as this," replied Klein, gesturing to Nathan's sweat-saturated gym clothes. His workouts were having an effect, his muscles showing through his increasingly tight shirt. "You gotta make sure you don't annoy the manager when you get back," he warned.

"Don't worry, I'll be twenty minutes, tops," replied Nathan.

"Have fun," mumbled a resigned Klein, waving his friend off as Nathan passed through the dormitory doors and into the night.

Nathan said he'd only run to the *Chickos* restaurant down the road. It would have only taken him twenty-minutes round trip. On the way through, he passed a field that was normally vacant at that time of night. But that night, it was hosting a late-night cricket game. His brow furrowed and his teeth chattered with uncomfortable flashes of memory. His legs tingled, and spurred him onward. He continued to run, passing the restaurant, and further down the street. Upsetting memories flashed incoherently across his mind, which drove him onward and distracted him. By the time he came to his senses, his legs were tired and feet sore. He tore off his shirt, saturated with sweat, and stuffed it in his back pocket. But the coolness of the night did little to help, and he fell on his backside, out of breath.

As Nathan recovered, his flashbacks subsided and he looked around. He realised he'd ran all the way to a warehouse lot in Unanderra. The place was deserted, and in the sparse overhanging nightlights, it seemed almost spooky. His gaze fell on one source of light, trickling through the doorway of one of the warehouses. It was old and decrepit, as if it had not been used in years. Curiosity drew him, and he stood to walk toward the warehouse.

The air inside the building reeked. The concrete was stained with splashes of brown, and Nathan could hear dripping liquid. His eyes adjusted to the faintness of flickering lights hanging from the roof above. His breathing hitched, as fear and foreboding infected his curiosity. He heard some strange sounds emanating from a darkened corridor nearby. Driven by lingering adrenaline from his run, Nathan crept toward the corridor.

A foul stench wafted from the opening, following the strange noises. They sounded like tearing and gurgling, and they grew louder as Nathan drew nearer. He stepped into the corridor and looked around. A ray of moonlight trickled into the room and glistened off a metallic shape. Nathan's eyes adapted to the dark and he saw the flash of razor sharp teeth, tearing voraciously at the flesh of a human body.

Nathan fell backward in horror, almost vomiting at the sight. His scream caught in his throat as his backside hit the soiled concrete. Realising the brown stains were dried blood, he scrambled away in panic. The thing in the shadows heard him and gave a guttural hiss.

Nathan sprinted as fast as he could to the exit and hid outside. His heart pounded with absolute terror. His eyes unfocused as he clutched his chest.

That wasn't real, he told himself. *I was just dreaming. I must be tripping.*

He heard sliding noises, like a heavy sack being dragged across the concrete. He edged his gaze around the corner, and looked into the warehouse. Something emerged from the shadowy corridor, but the light was faint and he couldn't make it out. He could see was that it was huge, and appeared to be made of metal. Its breathing reverberated through the warehouse with a chilling tone.

What is it?

His eyes widened and his horror multiplied, if that were even possible, at the sight of a figure walking through the warehouse. She appeared to be wearing a school uniform, but he couldn't make out what school. Her back was turned to the creature, and she seemed oblivious to its ravenously eager approach. The thing raised its tail as it drew near to her.

Without thinking, Nathan's legs whipped into action and he sprinted into the warehouse. He dove toward the girl, butting her out of the way with his shoulder, as the creature's sharpened tail burst through his chest.

Nathan woke with a start. He was on his back, in the middle of the block of warehouses. Confused, he grasped his chest, finding no hole where the creature stabbed him. He sat up and looked around. The warehouse he'd entered was empty and dark.

Maybe I just fell asleep here, he convinced himself.

Calming down, he stood up and stretched briefly. He stole one last look at the warehouse before beginning the run back to his dormitory.

Hopefully, the manager won't notice me coming back, he thought.

He did.

Nathan didn't seem any worse for wear the following morning as he finished his second helping of sugar-covered cornflakes before anyone was halfway through their first. Klein and their two other friends, Jessie and Paul, watched him gorge himself on cereal.

"Ah! Ain't no better way to start the day!" exclaimed Nathan.

"Ain't no better way to type two diabetes, either," said Klein through a yawn.

"You're not one to talk, lung cancer man," retorted Jessie with a jab of his spoon.

"Hey, popping out for a quick smoke ain't gonna kill me," said Klein. "What's more, obesity's the biggest killer for Australians."

Nathan just shot him a smirk and lifted up his shirt. "Cheese-grater!" he boasted as he indicated his muscles. They were indeed impressive.

A young girl, witnessing the display, marched over from the adjacent table and bellowed, "Nathan! Way to mess up your nice clean shirt!"

Nathan rolled his eyes, "Ariadne, it's not like you ironed it for me."

"That's no excuse!" chided Ariadne. "You're the elder, so you're supposed to set an example." Nathan sat there sardonically miming her words, but the girl didn't get a chance to berate him before Klein bellowed, "*This* is Ariadne!"

Her earlier rant gone to the darkest back of her mind, Ariadne swallowed, and veered slightly away from the boy.

"Umm … Who are you?" she asked.

"Klein Stevens," said the boy, his hand offered. "Nathan and I were buddies in junior primary. I knew you when you were really little." Ariadne couldn't bring herself to return the handshake, and instead just gauchely smiled as Klein rambled on. "Jesus, ain't you grown! I remember when you were teensy, and now look how cute you got!"

"Dude, she's twelve," said Nathan.

"I'm thirteen," interjected Ariadne.

"Twelve," Nathan insisted.

"I'm at least twelve and three quarters," Ariadne snapped. "I wouldn't be in Year Seven otherwise!"

"Oh yeah, the Year Seven's have their orientation today,

don't they?" said Jessie.

Ariadne began chirping about how excited she was to finally be at Warrawul. She was so excited; she wore the cutest grin on her face.

"Yeah, but be careful," said Paul. "You gotta make sure you obey the school rules, *and* the dorm rules." He motioned to Nathan. "Unlike your little brother here," he jibed.

"Older brother," Ariadne corrected.

"Yeah, but that's in body," said Jessie.

"So what about last night?" asked Klein. "Staying out all night better be worth Ol' Chambo busting you."

Nathan's brow furrowed as he sifted through the fragments of memory in his head. He decided not to mention why he ran way past the *Chickos* shop and made it all the way to Unanderra.

"I was kinda in the zone and just kept running," he said. "I got all the way to a bunch of warehouses in Unanderra. And, I must've passed out on the ground there. I had this dream that one of the warehouses had people in it. So I went to check it out and there was this thing in there. I was about to run, but then I saw this girl. It looked like she was about to get eaten by a snake. So I dove in."

Ariadne clapped her hands together and beamed. "And you saved her?"

"Nope, snake nailed me through the chest," said Nathan. Everyone either burst into laughter or palmed their faces in disappointment.

"You're supposed to save the damsel in distress, not get mowed over by the dragon," snapped Klein.

"Dude, not everything is like *World of Warcraft*," replied Nathan as he reached for the cornflakes a third time.

"Well, what did the girl look like?" asked Paul. "Maybe you might have seen her in real life?"

Nathan shrugged obliviously.

"What was she wearing?" asked Klein.

Nathan shot his friend a suspicious look. "Why?"

Klein grinned lasciviously. "If she was naked, then it was just a dream."

Nathan gave a dismayed scoff and pushed his friend away.

"Underage girls here, you dumbass," snapped Paul.

"The girl was wearing clothes, and it was a Catholic uniform I hadn't seen before," said Nathan, hoping to silence his friend as quickly as possible. At least that was successful, and Ariadne used it to change the subject. She gazed down at the yellow skirt and blazer combination with a smile.

"I'm so glad I finally get to wear this uniform," she said. "I remember when Nathan started at this school, and I wanted to go here too so I could wear the girls' uniform."

"Me too," exclaimed Nathan. "I too wished to wear the girl's uniform."

Ariadne gazed at Nathan blankly, a horrified chill mixed into that blankness. On the other hand, his friends simply rolled their eyes, except for Klein, who blurted indignantly, "So mentioning nude chicks is bad, but you're allowed to make cross-dressing jokes? What a hypocrite!"

"I'm trying to screw with *her*," replied Nathan as he pointed at his sister. She gasped a sigh of relief.

"Thank God, you're joking," she muttered. She looked to her brother's friends for confirmation, but found none. "He's joking, right?"

Nathan feigned a check of his watch and said, "Oh would you look at the time? Schools going to start soon."

He and his friends rose from the table, bussed their bowls, and waltzed out of the room with the rest of the crowd. Ariadne stood there, wide eyed, and yelled after them, "Please tell me you're joking!"

Ariadne and her friends eventually caught up to the convoy of boarders making their way to the school up the road. It was part way between the dormitories and the T-intersection where Mount Kiera Road meets the Highway. While her friends tried to assure Ariadne that her brother was just teasing her, Nathan chuckled at his ever-potent ability to mess with her mind. He wore a grin all the way to the school gates, past the off-highway car park, to his locker in the middle of the English classrooms. He'd barely punched in his combination before a dreaded voice pierced his good mood.

"I hear a disturbance was made in the dormitories last night," said the voice. Shivers of fear, frustration, and vexation clattered up Nathan's spine as he turned to meet the face of Ol' Chambo. And he did *not* look well. The colour had started to leave even his hair, leaving little more than dark green eyes through which he stared Nathan down.

"Mr. Chamberlain! Good morning, sir," said the boy.

"Disturbance. Dormitories. Nathan Grant," the teacher enunciated.

"Ah yeah, I figured the manager might've raised that," said Nathan. "Sorry, I needed to go for a run and I just went a bit too far. But it was a one-off thing, and it won't happen again. Cross my heart and hope to die."

"Maybe you might," murmured the teacher, and Nathan tried really hard to pretend he hadn't heard it. He jotted a few notes in a log, and then gazed at the boy again. "Detention will be at four-thirty. There are quite a few leaves clogging the storm drains behind the staffroom, and they need cleaning."

Nathan bent backwards with dismay and bellowed, "Oh, come on, mate. I've got assignments I need to work on."

"Plus this one," returned the teacher firmly. "Talk back, and I may add toilet cleaning to the duty list."

Nathan pursed his lips and acquiesced. After that, classes went slow, as they tend to do when the average school student stands at the start of the term. He imagined the next thirteen weeks stretch outwards to an infinite horizon. Of course, it didn't help that Nathan might not be getting back home until at least eight o'clock.

"I wonder why he's turned into such a tight-ass," mused Klein as he hoed into a meat-pie. The view from the roof of the science faculty gave quite a nice vista to enjoy one's lunch, but the mood was sullied by the news of Nathan's punishment.

"He used to be really nice," said Nathan. "It's only in the last couple of weeks, too, that he's become a real tosser."

Jessie snapped his fingers. "Maybe he got married, and the bride revealed herself to be Cruella De Ville!"

"Or Missus Bumble," added Paul, though the name earned him a few confused looks. "Seriously? Does no one read the prescribed English texts?"

Klein raised his fingers and counted down, "Three, two, one!" Then came the three-tenor chorus of, *NEEEEEERRRRD-AH!*

When the group sobered, Paul pointed out, "But isn't it weird? All the stuff that keeps happening? First, Asuna Yuki – you know, that Japanese girl who went missing. Then Teletha Testa-something. She goes missing too. Kids've been going missing quite a bit. The cops've been poking their noses around."

Klein shook off his shudders with a wave of his hand, "Ah, that won't matter. All they'll find from us is that Nathan's a trouser-lover, ain't that right?" He slapped Nathan on the shoulder to break him out of his musing, but all he got in return was a generic, "Yep!" that disguised how nervous the boy had suddenly become.

Afternoon classes finished, and a crowd of students trickled past their lockers on their way home. Nathan waved his friends off and trudged toward the staff building. The ladder and cleaning tools had already been laid out for him, and he set to work under Ol' Chambo's diligent gaze. The sun crept toward the horizon, and gave its ever-familiar shout-out of red and orange haze. Nathan watched it slowly disappear, and wondered if, somewhere, some other poor bastard was cleaning someone's gutters for nothing.

The last teacher left long before Nathan finished the job, and gave the boy a sympathetic look. Ol' Chambo stood dead still and fixated upon Nathan as if bearing some thousand-year-grudge soon to be sated. It wasn't much longer before Nathan threw his soiled, muddied hands in the air and exclaimed, "I'm done! I can't do anymore. Let the groundskeepers do it."

Ol' Chambo harrumphed and said, "Typical humans … Don't like doing something, just leave it to someone beneath you."

"Yep, I'm just a typical human!" said Nathan as he climbed down the stairs and marched straight up to the teacher. "And I'm done with this bollocks. All I did was go for a run, and I'm not workin' myself to death for it."

As Nathan marched off in the muddied remains of his uniform, Ol' Chambo chuckled.

"Sure you won't," he said. "Instead, you'll make the cattle do it. Or the mailroom boy. Or the poor bastard of indigenous descent with three kids he can't feed." Nathan stopped dead in his tracks, partially disturbed by the words and partially amazed that more than a monotone was leaving Ol' Chambo's mouth. "But there's always one thing you humans don't want to do, but can't pass off onto someone else … Die."

Nathan turned slowly and tried to keep his cool, but his Adam's Apple kept chugging up and down to wet his parched throat. "Nobody likes dying, Chambo."

"You, least of all, it seems," muttered the teacher as he sauntered toward the boy. "You dislike it so much, you simply refused to do it at my lair last night."

Nathan froze.

My lair … Last night … Refused to die.

"I was sure I skewered you through the heart when you got in my way," Ol' Chambo added, as his eyes grew brighter in the darkness. "My human anatomy is not that great, but I'm sure a heart is necessary. So, why aren't you dead?"

Nathan burst into laughter that was as strained as he was terrified. "Right, Chambo, great joke. Trying to scare me by saying that you'll kill me if I don't finish the job, right?

You're a real hoot, ya know?"

"Stop laughing," bellowed a deep voice that emanated menacingly from Ol' Chambo's throat. His mouth began to widen into a grin that was too large for his face, and it grew larger still. "It doesn't matter why you're still alive. I'll finish the job right now!"

A mass of tangled metal and frayed flesh burst out of the teacher's mouth. The mass clanged and contorted until it found its final form: a snake made of metal and mangled organs, three times as big as Nathan was tall. It's teeth, razor sharp, were identical to those he'd seen last night.

It roared as it lunged for him.

At the last moment, Nathan's legs found the sense to run. He darted around the buildings and sprinted faster than he had ever gone in his entire life. His every nerve tingled with adrenaline as he tried to avoid the monstrous beast. But it lithely slithered its way around the pillars and lockers Nathan tried to put between them.

Oh God! Oh God! Oh God! Oh God! I'm gonna die! I'm gonna get eaten by a cyborg snake that burst out of my teacher's mouth! I'm in Alien! That's what! I'm dreaming that I'm in a freaking Ridley Scott movie. Yeah! One of the older ones, before he sucked. And any minute now, I'll be saved! I'll turn the corner, and Sigourney Weaver will be there to save me!

He turned the corner, and actually found someone. Though this someone made his nightmare even worse!

"Whoa, Nathan! You scared me!" exclaimed Ariadne. "Not to mention, almost ran over me! What's the matter with you?"

Nathan's pale face was ghostly with horror. He looked over his shoulder, and found no snake after him.

Maybe it was just a dream after all? Maybe someone dosed me! No, I'm sure that just happened. I just got a head-start on it. But if it sees Ariadne ...

"What are you doing here?" he shouted with a husky tone.

"I came to see if you needed a hand with detention,"

replied Ariadne with a smile.

"You have to go! Now!" Nathan bellowed. His eyes darted around and found a pile of disturbed earth, skewered by a shovel. He grabbed the shovel and bellowed, "I'll hold it. Run and get the cops!"

Ariadne backed away nervously, and was sure it had to be yet another of Nathan's antics.

"What're you playing at now?" she asked. "What're you going to hold?"

She backed into what she thought was a tree, until her head clanged against something metal. She looked up, but not in time to see the jaws clamp shut around her. Nathan turned to see his sister's legs disappear down the snake's gullet like wriggling worms.

"Ah, now that was tasty!" bellowed the snake in the same deep voice.

Nathan, overwhelmed with shock, lunged and savagely swatted the snake's face with the shovel. Tears erupted from his eyes and flowed down his flushed cheeks as he screamed, "Give her back! Give back my sister! Give her back now!" Despite the adrenaline-fuelled blows he pounded on the snake's face, it didn't even flinch. When his arms couldn't swing any longer, he fell to his knees. "Please! Give her back!" he begged.

"Bored now!" mumbled the sarcastic snake. Its tail suddenly flicked against Nathan's side and sent him flying head-first into the trunk of a tree. It knocked the shovel out of the way with a sneer and uttered, "Try and kill a homunculus with a spade, will ya? My body was made by Alchemy, and nothing but Alchemy can unmake it."

Be it the concussion, the grief, or the fatigue, Nathan might never know. But that word, *Alchemy*, rung nostalgically in his head as if he'd heard it in a dream. His heart pounded with a mechanically toned thump, and a voice echoed in his mind.

You're dead, uttered the voice, announcing it as if it were the 'game over' sign on the TV. *You died because you dashed in, without knowing the situation or considering the consequences. Your family and friends will be grieved by your idiocy.*

His chest burned with agonising pain, and blood gurgled upward through his mouth. He let out strangled gasps for breath, his hazy gaze set upon the face of the girl who held him in his final moments. Her brow softened, and when it did, the long scar bisecting the bridge of her nose relaxed. She almost smiled, though it seemed rare for her.

That said, she went on, *you're a pretty interesting guy.*

She held up a hexagon made of silvery metal, Roman numerals etched into its centre-most surface.

This is Kakugane – Alchemy's ultimate alloy that resonates with the human soul, and gives form to our will to live. I can use this to replace your heart.

She pressed it into the place where his heart used to be, and he twitched and writhed in tremendous pain as the metal seemingly melded into his flesh with golden light.

With this, you will obtain a new life, and hopefully you'll take better care of it … For the sake of your loved ones.

Life began to flow through him again, more voracious and vivacious than ever before. It flowed so much it hurt more than dying, but only by a little.

To help you with that, the Kakugane will give you a new power: your soul, in the form of a weapon. When you are in danger, when you are about to lose that which you live for, then use it.

Nathan once again felt the hot breath of the snake as it loomed over him menacingly. Its tongue gave a predatory lash against his skin. He promptly swatted it away.

"Ooh, a bit more fight, have ya?" blurted the snake snidely. "You want your shovel back?"

Nathan dragged himself to his feet.

"I want Ariadne back," he growled.

The snake chortled, "Come and meet her in my gut."

"Shut the fuck up, you son of a bitch!" barked Nathan, and he glared defiantly into the creature's eyes. "You're giving back my sister!"

The ground beneath his feet shuddered and a whirlwind

gathered around his body. The snake withdrew, perturbed and intrigued by what was happening. A tremendous, triumphant roar blasted past Nathan's lips, and fuelled the tremors that reverberated around him. He placed his hand to his heart, and bellowed words he didn't know existed: "*Arms Alchemy!*"

Light burst from his chest in a vibrant cacophony of sound and radiance, all of which coalesced into a spear of shining silver and orange metal, arranged in patterns he could not have conceived had he been high on drugs. But he hadn't the time or the interest to consider the craftsmanship of the supernatural weapon.

He launched at the beast and slashed down its belly. The metallic flesh gave way like butter under a hot knife, and the snake collapsed in shock. Nathan panted a moment, reeling from the attack, and looked up to see a hand hanging from the wound, which tried to heal itself quickly. He dashed forward, grabbed the hand, and pulled with all his might. An unconscious Ariadne, covered in robotic entrails, followed the hand. Nathan held her tightly as the snake whipped its tail again and threw them against the wall.

"You scum! You realise how much energy it takes to heal?" roared the beast. "What kind of weapon is that?"

That same voice, belonging to Nathan's saviour, echoed from the roof of a nearby building, "He's a nosey guy, so a spear suits him."

The snake looked up to the roof, beheld its lost quarry, and growled, "You're the girl from last night."

The girl in the Catholic uniform shot out a sneer that would put Rambo to shame. She held up another hexagonal talisman. "Arms Alchemy! Valkyrie Skirt!"

The talisman caught fire with a blue shine, which girdled her hips and formed four robotic arms terminating in sharp blades. Before the snake could blink, she catapulted from the edge of the roof, directly toward the beast. She twirled sideways in the air, and her four mechanical arms made her a ballistic saw blade that sliced its way down the length of the creature's back. She hit the ground and bounced back the other way, and sliced the snake up like a salami sausage.

The creature wailed in agony with every slash of the blades, but the girl didn't let up. Eventually, all that was left was the head, the rest of it evaporating like water drops in a desert. The wretched thing tried to crawl away using its tongue as a grappling hook, but it didn't get more than a centimetre away before the girl's blade bisected it. The thing vanished unceremoniously before Nathan's eyes.

The girl turned to Nathan and stared at him.

"I got nothing," said Nathan flatly.

"Then you're proof Kakugane doesn't make you smarter," returned the girl. Her mechanical arms disintegrated into that blue light and returned to their inert, hexagonal form in her hand. "I see you learned how to use yours," she said, noting the spear in Nathan's hand. "And luckily you were able to save her life."

Nathan finally found the presence of mind to speak. "I tried to save you last night, but that thing killed me. What did it call itself?"

"Homunculus, a man-eating monster that disguises itself as a human … Oh, and I didn't need saving," said the girl.

"Come again?" Nathan muttered nervously.

"I'd set a trap for the dumb bastard last night," the girl snapped. "I was hunting it, you see. And you messed up the trap by trying to be cool."

"No way! I died for a misunderstanding?" the boy exclaimed. Tears nearly trickled from his eyes.

The girl took pity and walked over to him. She eyed the spear in his hand and gave him a smile.

"That said," she said. "You're a pretty interesting guy."

Nathan's cheeks flushed, and he involuntarily muttered, "I think I'm in love."

"What?" asked the girl, though by the tone of voice it was clear she'd heard his slip.

"Nothing!" Nathan choked. "What about my sister? We should get her to a hospital."

The girl eyed the drying goo covering Ariadne, and looked around her. Her eyes fell on the pile of dirt that harboured the shovel Nathan used before. She promptly picked up his sister and rolled her in the dirt.

"When she comes to, she'll assume she fell in some mud," explained the girl. "That's all you'll tell her, and that's all she'll know."

Nathan was flabbergasted. "What? You can't just say it's all a cover-up! What about all those knocked-over lockers?"

The girl scoffed, "Bugger if I know or care. That's not what I'm here for. I'm here to hunt homunculi."

"Well, didn't you just get it?" asked Nathan.

"Homunculi! *Plural!* There are a lot more than one in this town," retorted the girl. "Maybe you've been too busy watching cartoons at home, but people've been going missing in this town. Any idea why?"

Nathan suffered another flashback to mentions of names of kids who had disappeared from the dormitories.

She said they disguise themselves as humans, and eat people …

He gazed at his muddied, unconscious sister, lying on the dirt pile.

"Think about the chaos that would happen if people knew about these monsters," the girl went on with an urging tone. "Obviously, the police'll turn around and try to take the homunculi out. But as you've just seen, only weapons like ours will work. You and I, we have to keep this a secret."

Nathan hadn't heard a word she said, because he already knew her point. He grabbed his spear, planted it in the ground, and stood at attention.

"What should I do?" he asked.

"Take your sister home, and forget all of this," said the girl. "You can keep the Kakugane, but don't activate it ever again. I'll hunt down the rest of the homunculi in the town. Got it?"

"Bollocks!" barked Nathan. The girl's mouth fell agape. "I should have said, 'What do *we* do?'" The girl's expression turned confused. "Obviously, I'm going to help."

"Oh, no you don't," said the girl, backing away with her hands held up defensively.

"Come on!" exclaimed Nathan as he followed her. "I've got this awesome superpower and you've got one too. We'll be like a crime-fighting duo!"

"This is not a superpower!" barked the girl with a stab of her forefinger. "The Arms Alchemy is not a toy, and you can't use it to be a superhero. It's a curse."

"Bollocks it is!" Nathan protested. "You said it yourself: *when you're about to lose your loved ones, use it*. If there are more of those things in town – hell, even in our school! – I've got to use this weapon. No way am I going to sit back and not help."

The girl stood, wide-eyed and taken aback. Her face screamed with the need to make him go home, and more than once Nathan could see that she regretted giving him his new life. But the battle in her mind slowly came to a close, heralded by an acquiescent puff of her cheeks.

"Fine! You want to be like me, I'll take you on," she snapped. "I'll train you to be an Alchemic Warrior. But there are rules: no showing off to your friends; no comic book hero crap; and above all else … don't die again! Got it!"

Nathan straightened up and offered a wrong-handed salute.

"Yes, ma'am!" He gauchely added, "One more thing?"

"One more? What else do you want?" snapped the girl who looked like she'd had far too long a day.

"Umm … What's your name?" asked Nathan.

The girl stammered, "Oh, sorry. I forgot to tell you, didn't I? My name is …"

2 | The Butterfly Mask

"**A**strid Rachelle?"

Nathan lunged for his phone, tipping his breakfast over in the process. But Klein was much too fast for him, and darted out of the way to check the phone some more.

"Klein, give it back!" bellowed Nathan as he gave chase.

Klein was too filled with merriment at the situation to care for the murderous glimmer in his friend's eyes as he pranced around the food hall chanting, "Nathan's got a girlfriend!"

Paul managed to tackle the idiot and return the phone to its owner, but wasn't above demanding some details. "So who's this Astrid?" he asked.

Nathan shot his friends a hostile stare that belied how badly he wanted to keep his secret. But if there was one person who could read faces (if not minds), it was Paul Cuyper, and he knew something was up. He quickly gave up on the tight-lipped Nathan, and turned to another target at a girls' table nearby.

"Ariadne, what did Nathan get up to last night?"

Ariadne stopped eating mid-mouthful, and begrudgingly murmured, "Pushing me into mud puddles."

"I did not!" exclaimed Nathan. "You tripped and fell, remember?"

"You must've given me a concussion when you *pushed*

me," retorted the girl. "And after I came to help you …"

Jessie interjected, "Maybe he wanted to hide this Astrid from you."

Ariadne's ears perked up, "What Astrid?"

"Your future sister-in-law," said Klein with a chuckle. Ariadne squeaked excitedly, while the whole food hall reverberated with a salacious *'ooooooh!'* Nathan couldn't issue a comeback before his phone started ringing.

"Oi, he's talking to her now," said Paul, and the three boys and one sister tried to listen in. Klein's ears were sharper than the others and he heard him say, "Of course I won't tell people."

"Tell people what?" asked Klein, hovering over Nathan's shoulder. He continued to repeat the question like a broken record playing at chipmunk speed, until Nathan put the call on hold, grabbed him in a headlock and smacked his head several times.

"Sod off, you rotten bastard," he growled.

"Did you just slap me?" exclaimed Klein. "What are you, a sissy?"

"The biggest," returned Nathan sarcastically. "And trust me, if I used my fist, you'd be dead." He managed to finish his call in peace, outside the ear range of the eavesdroppers, and then came back to finish his upturned breakfast.

"So, where does this girl go to school?" asked Jessie, his own grin as blatant as Klein's.

"The Private School of Bite and Me," returned Nathan.

Ariadne fumed, "Oh come on! How could you not introduce her to me at least?"

"We've just joined the Inter-universal Cult of None-of-your-business," replied the boy, growing more furious.

"Maybe Astrid's really a guy," Klein murmured with every intention of letting Nathan hear it. Nathan readied his fist with bloodthirsty intent, and a cocky Klein said, "Come on then, show me Grant-Fu! Use your fist on me!" In the next instant, Klein was on the floor, nursing not a sore jaw but an aching groin. "You were right," he said with a high soprano. "I'm dead now."

Throughout the rest of the day, the group kept trying to coax an answer regarding this entity in Nathan's life, but he either remained silent or gave non-answers in the vicinity of, "She's an alien!" or "She's a secret agent!" or "She's Black Widow's daughter from a parallel universe!" By lunch it seemed they'd given up, but Nathan didn't consider that they were just biding their time.

The end of classes came, and Nathan was quickly out of the school and heading down the highway toward Unanderra. He stopped at the shops for a sausage roll (he got one for his new friend – if you could call her that), and then ran the rest of the way.

Oftentimes, Nathan would see these warehouses going past on a bus. He'd hardly paid it any mind. But today, he actually looked at the area in the sunlight. It seemed much less foreboding than it had the night before last.

He approached the old warehouse, which stood apart from the others currently being used. It was decrepit and looked more pathetic in the sunlight. It was a stark contrast to the other night, when he noticed the lights on inside and went to investigate … and get viciously and painfully murdered by a bio-mechanical basilisk.

Astrid stood just inside the decrepit building, leaning against a wall covered in peeling paint. In the daylight, he had a much better look at her. Her dark brown hair reached down to the middle of her neck and framed her face. The scar crawled from one cheek to the other across her nose, and to Nathan's sixteen-year-old brain it made her look bemusing, badass, and beautiful all at the same time. She still wore the Catholic uniform, though the shirt was slightly untucked from the skirt, and when the breeze blowed it slightly revealed a midriff that drove Nathan to instant distraction.

"Get enough sleep last night?" asked Astrid, but her blank face prevented Nathan from knowing if she was genuinely concerned or merely going through the motions of politeness.

"Yep," replied Nathan, his eyes still directed downward to her stomach. When Astrid asked what his problem was, he quickly bellowed, "Nothing! I'm just tired!" Not at all convinced, Astrid looked down and saw her slightly exposed stomach, and shot an irate glare at him. He apologetically held up the sausage roll as a peace offering, which she snatched with a brief whisper of, "Thanks."

They both went into the building and looked around. Astrid pointed out the bloodstains and bones on the floor, which made Nathan gag on his roll.

"This is – or rather, *was* – the homunculi nest," Astrid explained. "They'd kidnap people and bring them here for the rest of the hive to eat. When I came to this town, there were more than a dozen. Some of them were teachers, like your guy last night. Others were shop owners. One was even a kid at your school. I think her name was Asuna."

"Holy shit, I thought she had been eaten," Nathan exclaimed.

"Did you know her?" asked Astrid.

"Not really, only in passing," said Nathan.

"I'm sure she had friends …" the girl's gaze turned pensive. "But it was only a matter of time before she turned on them." She turned to Nathan and directed her fixed stare into his eyes. "I saved that girl's friends, just as you saved your sister. These things are heartless and brutal, the embodiment of evil. We have to destroy them all, or your friends will never be safe."

Nathan grunted approvingly and said, "I've already started toward that goal!" Astrid raised an eyebrow as Nathan reached into his bag, and pulled out a notebook. "This is my exercise regimen, to do every night! I've doubled what I normally do. Two hundred sit-ups, then two hundred push-ups, chin-ups, squats, followed by a ten kilometre run!"

Astrid face-palmed and exclaimed, "Do you take this remotely seriously?"

"Of course I do!" proclaimed Nathan. "I'm gonna get so strong that I'll be able to kill these Homer-Cumulous with a pinky finger!"

Astrid furiously snatched the notebook out of his hands and shouted, "You can't be serious when you say such stupid crap! Either that, or you still don't know what you're dealing with." Nathan's ears drooped sheepishly as his own stupid voice echoed in his head. The response only amplified her frustration. She pointed to a rickety flight of stairs. "Up there, now!"

As they climbed the stairs, Astrid asked, "I hope you at least looked up 'Alchemy' in the dictionary." She could have embedded the notebook in his head when she saw him grab his phone and say, "Google, what's Alchemy?"

The phone promptly replied, "*Alchemy: The medieval forerunner of chemistry, concerned with the transmutation of matter, in particular with attempts to convert base metals into gold or find a universal elixir.*"

Before Nathan could ask the phone what 'transmutation' meant, Astrid interjected, "That's only the common knowledge definition. All attempts to do that failed. The true forms of Alchemy, those are the ones that persist as one of the best-guarded secrets in the world. A thousand years ago, alchemists in Asia refined a rare metal with a property they'd never seen before: its form could mutate in response to the resonance of a human soul. It amplified the essence of the holder's mind and manifested it in a physical form. For most people, it was a weapon. With the Kakugane, the Alchemic Warriors were born, and sought to protect the world from evil."

"Let me guess," said Nathan, who grew giddy with the progression of the story. "The evil ones created hermi-clees, right?"

"Homunculi ... and no, they weren't necessarily evil, just stupid," said Astrid. "A little like you really. They just dove right in without considering the consequences. Homunculi were the work of European alchemists looking for immortality. And technically they succeeded. No ordinary weapons can kill these things, and so long as they keep properly nourished, they never senesce."

"Sen-what?"

"Die of old age," Astrid corrected.

Nathan hummed, trying to hide the information overload. "So where do they come from?"

Astrid led him through the corridors of the second floor to a room that smelled of rusted metal and dry soil. Amazingly, the light switch still worked, and it shed a dim, tired luminance over a series of benches. It was either the most complex or worst kept laboratory Nathan had ever seen. Recently used pumps sat diligently amidst the tangle of pipes and conduits through which they forced unknown compounds. All the conduits and machinery seemed to coalesce about a central scaffold that held an empty, pear-shaped test-tube.

"This is how you create a homunculus," said Astrid. "You extract cells from an organism – any organism – and culture them. Then you use the cell culture and an apparatus like this to grow an embryo based on those cells. It's a little like cloning, but not quite." She lifted the empty test-tube from the scaffold and gazed at it. "The embryo grows in here, until it is fully matured. Then it is ready to take a host."

Nathan shuddered, "A host?"

"A human victim," said Astrid darkly. "The embryo attaches itself to the body of a human and enters the brain. It then devours the victim, body and soul, and becomes a homunculus. The victim dies, and his or her skin becomes the guise for the newly-born monster within."

Nathan almost threw up his lunch in horror.

"So that means Ol' Chambo died and that thing took him over," he exclaimed. "And I assume the animal cells are what the thing can turn into?"

"Its true form, yes," said Astrid. She marched to the refrigerator nearby, and revealed chilled petri dishes full of multi-coloured growths. They were all labelled, but those labels were written in some Asian language neither Nathan nor Astrid could read. Nathan grabbed his phone, and opened the translator app.

"The text scanner on this sucks, but it should do," he said as he snapped a picture of the dish in her hand and checked the phone's analysis. "Apparently its Japanese. This one says 'lion.'" They scanned a few more: frog, eagle, rose, snake – "I guess we know who that was," Nathan murmured.

"There are twenty samples here," said Astrid. "Over the last few weeks, I snagged sixteen, including the snake. They're all here. I haven't found the frog, the eagle, the rose, or the lion yet."

"They must be the leaders then," said Nathan. "Since they're able to avoid you, they're obviously the smartest of the pack. So, they're the leaders."

Astrid grimaced as she gave it some thought.

"You're right," she said. "They are the smartest of the pack, and so harder to catch. But they aren't the leaders. Homunculi are no different, really, from the animals used to make them. They can't practice Alchemy; they can't even use the Kakugane." Nathan started to gaze around with a bemused face. "Think about it. Where did all this come from, if homunculi can't practice Alchemy?"

Nathan palmed his fist with sudden realisation.

"Someone else made them!" he exclaimed. "Someone else made all these samples and made the homunculi."

Astrid stabbed the air between them with her finger and said, "Exactly! We find the rest of the homunculi, and we'll find their leader."

Nathan roared excitedly and held up his fist to her. Astrid looked at it briefly, before his intent dawned on her and she bumped it gauchely.

"Let's kick some homunculus arse!" Nathan exclaimed, and marched out of the room. Astrid waited a moment and tried to restrain her smile, before Nathan returned and asked, "So, how do we find them?"

Astrid allowed herself a brief chuckle at his enthusiasm, before she pulled out her phone and showed him the recording app running on it.

"I planted a bug under the bench over there," she said. "It'll let me know when someone comes back."

Nathan giggled like an excited kindergartener. "You really are a secret agent! It's like, 'Astrid Rachelle, beautiful and badass!'"

Astrid pocketed her phone and sighed, "Stop hitting on me. It's creepy." She left the room, with Nathan in tow.

The boy defended his words, "I wasn't hitting on you. I was giving you a complement." Astrid shushed him. "Seriously, you can't be that shy."

"Quiet!" she shouted in a whisper. "Something's on the roof."

The pair scrambled up the rest of the stairs and burst onto the roof of the warehouse. There, on the highest part of the building, stood two figures. The first was an aboriginal man in a trench coat. He had windswept hair and a yellow-eyed glare so keen it would put a sniper to shame. Behind him stood a tall, slender being wearing an extravagant butterfly mask, and a Warrawul school uniform.

"I always thought Alchemic Warriors would be older," said the masked man with a clearly fake Italian accent.

"That's a uniform from your school," whispered Astrid.

"You're the one who runs the lab, aren't you?" Nathan bellowed. He eyed the green necktie. "You're a Year Twelve student too."

"I'm far from the average school student, mind you," said the masked man.

"Master, shall I engage?" murmured the aboriginal.

"Patience, Burrumering," said the masked man. "Let us try a more polite approach."

A hand flew into the man's blazer and threw another pear-shaped test-tube. It shattered at Astrid's feet. Astrid leapt back more horrified than Nathan, whose gaze caught the tiny grey thing that hurtled upwards from the ground toward her. It writhed in the open air, feebly clawing and squealing at its quarry. Without a single word, those bladed arms erupted from Astrid's hips and slashed at the creature in a panicked flurry of swipes. The thing deflected from the blades, flew over her head, and off the roof to the ground below.

"Astrid! Are you alright?" Nathan exclaimed.

"Never mind me!" barked the out-of-breath girl. "That embryo won't survive much longer without a host." Her robot arms flexed as she assumed a fighting position. "Get ready."

Nathan tried not to sound giddy as he placed his hand to his heart and roared, "Arms Alchemy!"

The spear materialised in his hand, complete with a long red sash that flowed from the hilt. Nathan's giddiness reached childish levels as he exclaimed, "Hey, check it out! I hadn't noticed this cloth before!"

"Focus, you idiot!" barked Astrid. Nathan assumed an amateurish fighting stance, and steeled himself. Astrid glared at their opponents and yelled, "Let's finish this!"

The masked man pompously palmed his face, and intoned, "Oh, I do wish you'd be my latest experiment, but no matter."

Burrumering inhaled sharply, and his flesh contorted gracefully into a magnificent bird of black and gold. His metallic feathers ruffled as the masked man climbed onto his back and said, "Devour them."

The eagle swooped down over them and knocked them onto their backs. Astrid countered with her blades, but the beast swiftly dodged her strikes and seemed to vanish. It glided around the building and came back for another assault. Nathan prepared himself, and jumped to strike. The creature pitched and the spear hit air.

"Stop treating it like an ordinary weapon!" barked Astrid. "It's your soul! It will respond to your will."

Nathan landed near the edge of the roof and almost fell off. He steadied himself and watched Astrid try to slash the enemy that darted out of her reach. The robotic arms that extended from her hips seemed to act as if they were part of her body.

Like that bad-guy in Spiderman, she controls those arms with her mind, he realised.

Burrumering soared into the air beyond their reach, and then began a steep dive toward them. Nathan glanced at his spear and the sash, and had an idea.

"Astrid, grab onto the sash," he said. Astrid clutched the long red cloth, and Nathan took aim at the incoming creature. He summoned a tremendous roar from his gut, and the sash flashed gold as he threw the spear. It did exactly as he imagined, and flew straight into the air and took Astrid with it. The blade glanced the eagle's face, and gave Astrid a clear shot at the masked man on its back.

"Gotcha now, ya bastards!" she screamed, and willed the blades through him. At the last instant, the eagle darted away, and vanished in a streak of light. As gravity reclaimed her, she gazed out to the horizon to where the creature fled.

I've never fought one like that, she thought. *That thing is on a whole different level.*

Nathan rushed to catch her as she fell, and ended up running into the wall of the uppermost roof. He fell backward, dazed, and was almost skewered by his own spear as it hit the ground very near his head. Astrid hit the upper roof, absorbed the recoil with her blades, and then gracefully flipped through the air. She hit the floor in front of him with a vintage superhero landing as her Kakugane rematerialized in her hand.

"Oh my god, that is so unbelievably cool!" Nathan screamed. He began dancing around like a child with a new toy. "My first real fight! Howzat? I threw my spear in the air and it did exactly what I wanted it to. And then you land like some badass chick out of an action flick and, *OH MY GOD!* This is so cool."

He repeatedly verbalised his excitement until he was out of breath, and collapsed on the ground. Astrid just looked at him with folded arms and pursed lips.

"Finished?" she asked.

"For now," he mumbled.

She kneeled down to him and looked him squarely in the face. "Nathan, this isn't a game! Either one of us could have died. *I* could have turned into a monster myself, and *you'd* have had to deal with me. Don't you get that?"

"Sure I do," said Nathan, his grin still there. "But we lived, didn't we? And we kicked that *Papillon* guy's arse!" Astrid shot him a confused look. "Papillon, it's French for 'butterfly.' You know, the mask he was wearing?"

Astrid rolled her eyes. "You're having fun," she said.

"How could I not?" replied Nathan. He sat up and looked at her with star-speckled eyes. "I'm fighting monsters and saving my friends while I'm at it. It's freaking awesome!"

Astrid could not recall any Alchemic Warrior, be it professional or rookie, who greeted the job like this boy. His cockiness seemed infectious as she laughed, "God, you're weird."

Nathan launched to his feet.

"Come on, we need to take care of that embryo," he said.

"That's no problem," said Astrid. "It won't survive long when exposed to air." Then her eyes darkened. "There is something else we need to take care of."

Five minutes later, the pair strutted out of the building, leaving behind a wrecked laboratory smattered with frayed wires and shattered glass. Luckily, their weapons were safely stowed in their inert forms, or four overly nosy pairs of eyes might have discovered their secret. Instead, those eyes found only that which they thought was the real secret.

"Ah! Nathan's really got a girlfriend!" screamed Ariadne like an infantile gossip columnist.

Astrid almost choked on her tongue.

"And she's a hottie!" exclaimed Jessie.

Both Nathan and Astrid turned away quickly, and she murmured to him, "What're their names? Don't point out which one's which, just the names." Nathan gave them, and Astrid promptly twirled. She put on a friendly smile that was so alien on her face Nathan almost found it creepy.

"Hi!" she exclaimed with the most chipper voice. She approached them and said, "It's nice to meet you! Nathan's told me so much about you all."

"Funny, he hasn't mentioned you much at all," said Paul with an interested glance at the girl's apparel.

Astrid turned back to him and chirped, "Oww, have you been shy?"

Nathan could only yammer and stammer in bewilderment. Klein gave a holler and marched up to him to slap him on the back.

"It's good to see all my training has paid off!" he bellowed.

"Ah! My big brother's got a pretty gal!" screeched Ariadne as she pounced on the girl. She promptly introduced herself, and left Nathan to introduce the others.

"Never mind the intros! What the hell're you doing at this cruddy dump?" asked Klein.

"Oh, Nathan and I are scouting this place for the next paintball tournament," said Astrid with a wave of her hand.

Ariadne's eyebrows rose, "Since when are you into paintball, Nathan?"

Be it that the time he had to process Astrid's sudden character change, or some miraculous switch falling into place in his head, Nathan finally caught onto the ploy and said, "Oh yeah, I was walking through the Figtree Grove and Astrid was selling paintball membership. So I figured, why not?"

"Was a bit of effort to get him involved on my part though," said Astrid. "Had to practically push the membership form on him."

"Yeah, Nathan loves the gym but you really can't get him into sport," intoned Klein.

"Oh, maybe we shouldn't have interrupted your scouting," said Jessie.

"No, it's fine, we're finished," said Astrid.

Paul finally pulled his interest away from Astrid's uniform and suggested they all go for a drink, to get to know the new arrival to their group. Ariadne was thrilled at the idea, and Astrid seemed even more thrilled.

"Sure, let's go get a drink," she said with an unexpected spike in the pitch of her voice.

The group started walking, Nathan and Astrid lagging behind. He leaned down to her and asked, "Did you have a stroke or something?"

"I can act when necessary," she murmured, her usual business-like tone having returned with a dash of heightened nervousness.

Nathan traced her gaze, fixated on his little sister. He finally saw what bothered her so much: a sinister-looking thing, the size of a tiny lizard, clinging maliciously to Ariadne's ponytail.

He almost screamed, *The homunculus embryo!*

3 | The Hunt

The thing trembled as it ascended yet another agonising millimetre up the rope that was Ariadne's ponytail. Thankfully, though amazingly, the girl didn't notice the tiny lizard resembling a cross between a cyborg's vomit and the Cloverfield monster. It mustn't have been that heavy, or Ariadne's ponytail was so tightly done that she couldn't feel it.

What the hell am I thinking about? Nathan inwardly screamed. Astrid was far more composed, but that wasn't saying much as cold sweat trickled down her brow. She quickly threaded her fingers into Nathan's and leaned up to him.

"Let me handle this," she said. "You don't have enough practice with your Arms Alchemy, so you can't activate it without a verbal command. My Valkyrie Skirt is quiet and precise. I won't let anything happen to your sister."

"Just make sure you don't cut her accidentally," Nathan replied.

Suddenly, Klein yelled over his shoulder, "Oi, no smoozin' behind your mates' backs, Nathan."

At that, everyone, including Ariadne, turned around to see them holding hands. Nathan's sister giggled delightfully, "Ooooh! Look at them getting all lovey dovey!"

The looks on their faces were difficult to comprehend, and none of the friends could tell if they were embarrassed, angry, or scared. But it didn't seem to matter to the friends, as they'd already decided what was in Nathan's head.

"Yeah, no making out behind us," said Jessie.

"If you're gonna make out, at least let us watch, eh?" added Klein with playful leer.

God-bloody-damn it, you idiots!

That was the thought streaming through both Nathan and Astrid's minds. Astrid noticed Klein's eyes dart slightly, and her heart skipped a beat.

"Hey, Ariadne, you got a lizard in your hair," he said.

Ariadne, being the fretful girl she was, suddenly swivelled around as if to see the back of her head. The hair swung outward with enough force to break the embryo's grip, and it flew straight at Nathan.

The little girl fumbled through her ponytail, and Paul helped steady her to look for the little creature.

"Hey, it's gone," said Paul. "Sure you saw something?"

Klein shrugged, "I guess I was seein' things. Never mind. Now, let's get goin'!" His eyes went to the footpath behind them. No one was there.

"Where are they?" asked Jessie.

Klein let out a frustrated growl, "Soddin' bastard! Ditches his mates to run off with his girlfriend."

"It does kinda suck when a friend gets a girl, doesn't it?" intoned Jessie.

"Well, they might want their space," said Ariadne, though she was just as disappointed as her brother's friends. "I wanted to get to know her too."

Paul just straightened his glasses quietly, and mumbled, "She was wearing a Catholic uniform."

* * *

Nathan woke with a gigantic lump on his head, and when he stood up, gravity pulled him from three directions at once, none of which were down. Of course, he couldn't really tell which way was down.

"Did someone spike my drink?" he mumbled.

"Nope, you've got a concussion," came the sultry sound of Astrid's voice.

Nathan was so delirious, his internal censor failed and he murmured, "What kind of naughty thing is that?"

He got a palm to his face, which helped him wake up a little more. He sat up, his head still splitting with pain, and looked over to see Astrid. She straightened out her skirt, which clued Nathan into the possibility that he'd been resting his head on her thighs. They still had a red indentation from his head, and by the way she stood he could tell they were a little sore.

Happy times, roared his concussed brain. Or maybe it was his hormones. Whichever was thinking for him eventually collected itself enough to ask, "What happened?"

"Probably the head bump," murmured Astrid as she gingerly sat on a tree stump in the middle of the clearing, and gently rubbed her stomach. "We're in the ravine near the Avenue. I pushed you down here. Sorry about that."

Nathan's brow furrowed, and flashes of his sister's flicking hair strands barged into his subconscious. His eyes widened in panic.

"Ariadne!" he exclaimed over the screech of his headache.

"She's fine," said Astrid. "So are your friends."

Nathan sighed with relief. "Sorry about them. They didn't know what was happening. At least that embryo didn't get them."

Astrid grimaced at the comment, and when Nathan saw her crossness, she lifted her shirt. Nathan's tummy fetish vanished along with his presence of mind to breathe. Just to the right of her navel was a tumorous mass with sinister, lidless black eyes. It pulsated as its entire lower body sank meticulously into her flesh. Its arms, legs, and tail had become veiny tendrils that melded with the inflamed skin at a languid, almost sadistic pace. The embryo quivered as Nathan drew near to it, as if to shout, "My turf! Get lost!" And when it did, Astrid screamed. With overwhelming will, she bit it back to a soft whimper.

Nathan looked up at the girl, speechless. Her brow only slightly tensed, and he wondered how much pain she was actually in. A tiny sliver of memory crept into his mind of that thing flying toward him, then her in front of him, and then both of them tumbling down the hill.

"You took it for me," he said. "It's gonna turn you into a monster, isn't it?"

"I'm lucky it didn't hit my head, otherwise I'd've been a homunculus before we hit the ground," she grumbled. "At least with this, there's a chance."

"A chance?" exclaimed Nathan.

"I just hope that Papillon isn't so much of an idiot to not have a just-in-case," said the girl.

Nathan was confused, since 'just-in-case' meant something very different to the Year Ten boys of Warrawul Boarding School.

"How will *that* help?"

"In case he makes a mistake with his experiments and the embryo bonds to him," said Astrid. "He should have a cure on hand, *just in case.*" Nathan's eyes widened with understanding before grimacing sheepishly. Astrid's eyes narrowed, "What did you think I meant?"

Nathan just laughed and said, "Never mind. Anyway, so all we have to do is find Papillon and get the cure from him. He's obviously a student at the school, and a Year-Twelver too. We'll just ask around for an Italian kid, no problem!"

Astrid grinned, "You really over-estimate how easy things will be."

"*Over-estimate* is my middle name," said Nathan, matching her smile.

Nathan shouldered Astrid up the hill and out of the ravine. Soon they were back where they left their friends before, but it was night out. It really was a shame that their first night out was spent hobbling back to the dormitories, with a man-eating monster clawing its way along Astrid's skin.

Hell, first time I see her belly button, I'm more distracted by the world's worst tick, Nathan thought.

If only the highway leading to the dormitory wasn't so heavily lit. Otherwise, Nathan would be able to look up and see the stars, and it would feel at least slightly romantic.

Come on, dude, you shouldn't be thinking about that. She just pulled a Kevin Costner for you.

They reached the dormitories. Most of the students were in their rooms studying or chatting away. The pair went into the common room, sparsely populated by kids too enthralled in the latest episode of some TV show to notice them. They went to the back shelf, where the first aid stores could be found with the Panadol and the epi-pens. Nathan bandaged over the homunculus embryo, which thankfully didn't seem to mind being covered. Either that, or Astrid was just covering up her own distress. When they were done, they sat down on one of the couches some distance away from the TV.

Astrid eyed the kids who took only the slightest notice of her, and thought aloud, "Not everyone will notice me here, but at the school, I'll be a lot more conspicuous."

"Maybe I can get Ariadne to lend you her uniform," Nathan intoned.

"How will you convince her?" Astrid asked with a sceptical raise of the eyebrow.

"I'll ask her nicely," replied the boy with a smile.

At that moment, Ariadne entered the room and glared at her brother.

"Nathan! Where the heck did you two get to?" she bellowed, ignoring the jeers and shushes from the kids enthralled with the TV. Nathan just launched to his feet and hugged his sister. The overwhelmed girl looked at him incredulously and mumbled, "What was that for?"

"For being such a wonderful sister!" exclaimed Nathan. His smile was infectious, and she forgot her earlier irritation. Nathan went on, "Ariadne, can I borrow your uniform, please?"

Ariadne went pale. "Why?"

"Astrid and I need it for something," Nathan said blatantly.

A second later, the girl was gone, having left horrified teardrops on the floor and a red hand-print on Nathan's cheek. As he sat down, he looked at Astrid, who offered him a bewildered look mixed in with the same kind of discomfort that was blatant on his fleeing sister's face.

"Even I know that sounded creepy," she murmured.

"But I was being nice," Nathan retorted, clearly oblivious. "But how will you sneak around the school now?"

"You've got a sport uniform, right?" asked Astrid. "I'll just wear the tracksuit."

Nathan shrugged, "I guess that works."

"I'll probably have a week, tops, before this thing gets to my brain," said Astrid as she rose to her feet. "In that time, we can find Papillon. But if we are to fight him, we'll need to get past that eagle homunculus. Burrumering, he was called. He's no ordinary monster." Her eyes looked Nathan up and down, and she continued, "We'll search the school by day, and at night, I'll train you. When we find Papillon, we'll be ready."

Nathan stood and looked fixedly at her.

"Sounds like a plan," he said.

* * *

Though Nathan's sport tracksuit hardly fit her small frame, Astrid blended in at the school fine. So long as Nathan's friends never saw her, she was free to scan the classes as she liked, pretending to be working for the student council and taking a census of the school.

She offered a description of Papillon to people she spoke to during recess and lunch, and looked around the Year Twelve rooms during class. But no one matching the description turned up.

Nathan had equally dismal luck, as no one could think

of a person remotely like the one Astrid described.

"The mask didn't really help much," said Nathan as they trudged out of the school after classes. "All we've got to go on is the shape of the smile and the eyes."

"Trust me, you'll know when you see him," said Astrid. "Dark green eyes, jet black hair, and the smile you'd expect of a sociopath."

Nathan scoffed, "You must watch more movies than I do."

"No, I've just had more psych training than you," said Astrid.

"Where did you get psych training?" Nathan asked as he stifled a defeated yawn.

"The agency I work for," replied Astrid. "There are way many more Alchemic Warriors than just us."

Nathan glared at her incredulously, "Why not ask them for help?"

"Already have, and they said they'd have someone out there as quickly as possible," Astrid replied. "But most agents are locked up on other assignments. Homunculi aren't the only problem the agency faces, mind you. There're also a rogue alchemists, like Papillon. Also witches."

"Witches? What, like Hermione Granger?" interjected Nathan.

"No, like walking nukes with nothing resembling a conscience," replied Astrid. "And I'm part of one organisation dealing with them, and there aren't as many as there really should be."

Nathan huffed, "So we're alone?"

"For now," said Astrid. She grabbed his hand, "Come on, we need to get training."

Nathan dropped his bag off in his dorm room, and tried to escape the gazes of his friends as he darted out of the building. That first time, Klein saw him and gave him a thumbs-up.

"Go mate," he encouraged. "Oh, and make sure you got

your *just-in-case.*"

"We're not gonna do that," was what Nathan wanted to say, especially considering the volume with which his friend cheered him on. Instead, he just smiled over his shoulder and returned the thumbs-up. He and Astrid met at the building gates and walked to the abandoned warehouse at Unanderra.

There were still no signs that anyone had been there, and the lab was still a wreck.

"Just like we left it," said a satisfied Astrid. She winced, as if the embryo heard her and didn't like her tone. Then she took her Kakugane out of her pocket and turned to Nathan. "Let's get started." She said nothing, and the Kakugane luminously transformed into her robotic scythes. She winced even harder when the transformation was complete.

"You alright?" asked Nathan.

"Yeah, it just doesn't like the scythes," replied a panting Astrid. She quickly composed herself. "We can still train. Now, you need to learn how to summon the Arms Alchemy without a word, just like I did. The reason it works when you yell is that it responds to fighting and survival instincts. When you yell, you release adrenaline, which the Kakugane responds to. You need to learn how to yell with your thoughts."

Nathan nodded, closed his eyes, and tried to think.

Fighting instincts, activate!

Nothing happened.

Arms Alchemy!

Still nothing.

Come on, man! You've got to get good so we can get the cure for Astrid. She's in so much pain because of you. That thing is right next to her belly button, eating away at her wonderful chiselled abs. Oh, goddamnit! Here I am, fantasising about her tummy, and can't think straight!

"What's the matter?" asked Astrid. Nathan's eyes flew open and he fumed with frustration. "You need to be focused exactly on what you want."

"I am focused on what I want!" returned the irate boy. "I just keep getting distracted."

"Then you're not focused," replied Astrid. "I was watching you. You got this silly grin all over your face. Thinking about something funny on TV?"

"I was thinking about your belly button," said Nathan absentmindedly. A quartet of blades found themselves veering close to several of Nathan's vital body parts. Astrid glared at him with a look that screamed of dwindling patience.

"Maybe I should threaten you with death, then?" she growled. Nathan's lips cracked a nervous smile. "Stop smiling! This isn't a joke! Maybe I should have let that snake have you. Then I wouldn't have to deal with you or your friends."

Blood drained from Nathan's face, and he thought back to the monster hiding in Ol' Chambo's body. Without any permission from the rest of his mind, he began to envision such a beast appearing before Klein, or Paul, or Jessie. He imagined, with vehement protest, a beast whose fangs dripped with blood as they sank into his sister's body – a beast whose face resembled Astrid.

Astrid's scythe blades were thrown aside, and she darted back quickly to avoid the swipe of Nathan's spear, which appeared in his hand with neither a flash nor a shout. The boy held the lance threateningly. His face was pale with rage and fear as he panted. Astrid trembled, as if her stamina had been cut. But she was impressed, and rose to her feet to look at him.

"*That* is being focused," she said. "Seeing what you want and knowing how to make it happen. That is the true power of the Arms Alchemy."

Nathan shuddered as he gripped the lance, which pulsed with faint internal light. He said, "It's scary stuff."

"It is," said Astrid as she gazed at her scythes. "But I will teach you to control it." The embryo twitched beneath her shirt, and she inhaled sharply like she'd been burned. Nathan looked at where she gripped her stomach, and then to the lance in his hand.

I will stop these things, he thought. *I have to.*

With a cocky smile, Nathan bent down and said to Astrid's stomach, "Complain all you want, you son of a bitch."

* * *

By the fourth day, the duo had checked the whole of Year Twelve three times, and still no one turned up matching the description. It was particularly annoying for Nathan. According to Astrid, he was improving with his training, but he chalked it up to the homunculus embryo handicapping her. Adding insult to injury, his sister had been avoiding him since the third day.

"It's not my fault," said Nathan when discussing it with Astrid over training. "You had my sports tracksuit, so I asked to borrow hers."

Astrid face-palmed and said, "Are you *trying* to traumatize your sister?"

Nathan grinned evilly, "Next, I'm gonna invite her to Mardi Gras."

"You can't be serious!" exclaimed Astrid.

"Sure I can, I just don't want to be," replied the boy with a grin Astrid couldn't help but match.

At the end of the school week, they made their way toward Unanderra for more training. As they walked, Nathan hung his head in defeat.

"If we keep asking about this guy, the teachers'll get suspicious," he droned. "My mates are already getting a little nosey."

Astrid stopped walking and turned to him. "Maybe you should take a break tonight."

"What about training?"

Astrid shrugged, "We've done that every night all week. We both need a bit of a re-charge. And you're right, your friends are gonna get a little suspicious if you're always hanging around with your girlfriend." Nathan blushed, and Astrid rolled her eyes, "You know what I mean. Go home. I'll call you tomorrow."

Nathan revealed his fatigue with a slump of his shoulders and acquiesced. He turned and began the walk back to his dormitories.

Fancy that, he thought. *She's only got two days or so before that thing finishes her. And she's letting me have a night off. Not that I don't mind a break. I was starting to get tired … Maybe I should shout her something, just to say thanks.*

He turned around and walked back down the path. He turned a corner and found Astrid, but before he could call out to her, his breath hitched at what he saw. Astrid slumped against a wall for what little support it offered. She panted heavily, and her stifled sobs of agony were audible from a distance. She took a deep breath and growled to summon her strength, and then walked down the path and out of sight.

"Poor girl must be sick," said a British sounding voice behind Nathan. He turned and saw a man in his late thirties. His hands rested in the pockets of his worn out leather jacket, which hung about his stout form. His beady eyes gazed past Nathan as if he wasn't standing there, and shot a fixed glare down the path Astrid had walked. At first, Nathan paid him little mind, until he caught the lustful shimmer in the man's eyes. It was just like the sinister look Ol' Chambo gave off in the last minutes of his life.

The man groaned wantonly, "Master says she's gonna be one of us, but it'd be such a waste. Look at all that. What soft tender flesh she must have?" The man began to drool. Nathan couldn't move, though whether he was immobilised by fear or anger he didn't know.

"So young, so fresh," the man moaned. Then he said defiantly, "I must have her, with chips, gravy, and a nice pint of beer."

That set Nathan off.

"You stay away from her," he snapped.

The man finally looked down at him and said, "What're you gonna do to stop me? I've been watching you train, if you could call it training. I could snap your neck and not show a glimmer of my true form."

Nathan wasted no time, gripped the man's shoulders, and kneed him in the groin with all his strength. The man hobbled away slightly, doubled over and groaning softly.

"Below the belt, I know, but you really shouldn't screw with me," said Nathan triumphantly. "Now tell me where your master –"

"Psych!" exclaimed the man with a grin. He tackled Nathan, and they both fell down the hill beside the road. They reached the bottom of the hill, bruised and battered by the fall. The man threw Nathan off him and leaped to his feet with all the spryness of an Olympic athlete. He ripped his jacket away, and his flesh quivered and ruptured. It secreted folding metal that grew organically to consume his outer shell of human disguise, and revealed a mechanical toad. Its copper carapace glimmered in the failing light, as it's eyes flashed with sinister rage.

"Since I know you go for the bollocks, I know what kind of guy you are," he bellowed. "You're a push-over! A wimp! I'll kill you, eat that delectable morsel, and take your Kakugane. Then I'll be the master!"

Nathan glared at the thing before him, his lips pursed into a sneer of pure determination. He wouldn't have the element of surprise like he did with Ol' Chambo, but he had more experience. And he knew exactly what he wanted.

"You know what happens to a toad when it's struck by lightning?" he asked. The beast cocked its head. Nathan then bellowed, "Nothing as bad as getting your arse kicked by me!"

His hand to his chest: "Arms Alchemy!"

4 | The Toad and The Rose

"That'll be twenty-fifty, thanks," said the cashier. Klein scooped up his bag full of powerade, chips, and the latest copy of *Zoo* magazine, and hopped off back toward the dormitories.

It's good that Nathan's got himself a girl, he thought. *Now he won't steal my mags and spill coke all over them.*

The path inclined down as he walked past the school, and he recalled something Paul had mentioned a few days back.

Astrid was wearing a Catholic uniform ... Really though? I dunno what a Catholic uniform looks like. But if he had a dream about her ...

He stopped dead in his tracks, and almost burst a blood vessel as he belched, "He was gettin' it with her before we met her! And he stole my mags all weekend last week!" He gazed down at the magazine in the bag, and almost shed a tear for the full-busted lady on the front cover. "Don't worry, you poor dal. I won't let that perve get anywhere near you." He picked up his pace, all while mumbling to himself. "Rotten bastard! That hot girl should be enough for him."

"Enough for who?" came a voice that pierced his mind. The stern face of Astrid stared back at him.

"Hey! Astrid! How's it going?" exclaimed Klein, trying not to empty his bladder in shock.

"I'm fine," said Astrid with a wary gaze. "Are you

alright? You look a little pale."

"I'm *tanfastic*," said Klein breathlessly. "Just coming back from the shops."

Astrid gauged the bag's contents in an instant. She offered him a raised eyebrow, "Photoshopped pictures of pretty girls?"

The bag suddenly vanished behind Klein's back, and he withdrew suspiciously from the girl.

"This is mine," he exclaimed. "Nathan ain't gettin' his pervy hands on my girly mags, got it? It should be enough that he's got a hot girlfriend."

Astrid cocked her head, confused a moment as to who this girlfriend was. Then she gave a scoff of realisation and sighed with annoyance. Klein looked at her, a little confused himself by her demeanour.

"Look," he said. "If we're makin' you two uncomfortable at all, sorry. No need to be shy, I was just havin' fun."

The girl shot a bewildered look at him, as if she was even more embarrassed, but at the same time unsure if her shame was necessary. She pushed past her awkwardness, and said, "I'm just heading to the dorms to return something to him. Any chance you could give it to him?"

Klein finally noticed she had a plastic bag of her own.

"Oh, so you're buyin' him mags now?" he said without thinking. Astrid's eyes screamed murder, and Klein looked at the bag again. "His tracksuit?"

"I borrowed it for something," said Astrid. She promptly choked as she realised what that could mean. "I'm just returning it!"

Klein threw his hands up defensively, "Hey, whatever. But I don't think he's back yet. I only stepped out about five minutes ago, and he wasn't there. It's weird, since Ariadne hasn't been able to contact him either."

If Klein had been looking at Astrid's face, he'd have seen her expression crumple with fear and concern. The tracksuit fell to the ground as she turned and sprinted down the path.

By the slight limp in her gait, Klein thought she'd torn a muscle.

"Oi, Astrid! What's the matter?" he called after her, but she was gone too quickly. He picked up the bag with the tracksuit, and his brow crinkled with curiosity.

I know Nathan's a bit of a weirdo, but I can't believe that tracksuits would turn him on. And the Catholic uniform. Plus, he's out, but not with Astrid.

Then a realisation dawned on him.

Oh, he better not be sleazin' it with multiple girls. That's not cool.

He gave chase.

* * *

A hail of red metal buffeted Nathan, and he barely escaped the brunt of the homunculus' attack. He fell backward, and darted out of the way as the frog brought his tongue down like a whip. The strike flattened the earth with a crack that sent chills up his spine.

The frog eyed him snidely.

"This all ya got?" it murmured as its whip-like tongue lapped at its lips. Nathan panted, exhaling in staggered, shaky strokes as he strove to control his own trembling nerves.

So much for training, he thought amidst his fear-addled impulses to run screaming.

"I've got the best eyesight of my brethren, ya know?" the frog went on. "I was able to watch you from a mile away when you and my next meal were *training.*" Two webbed pairs of fingers twiddled the air either side of its head as it uttered the word. It cracked a smile that betrayed more disappointment than amusement.

Nathan launched another attack with his spear, bringing a haymaker aimed for the frog's left. It dodged the blow and swiped to the right. Like the frog, Nathan could only dodge, but he was hardly as flexible as he assumed he'd be, and couldn't arch his back enough to escape the attack. It contacted his cheek and he spun in mid-air before striking the ground hard. The tongue flew toward him again, but this time he rolled fast enough to escape, and he swiped an arc with his spear. The frog darted out of the way, which was entirely its mistake as it missed what suddenly mesmerised Nathan.

The intricate seams of the spear split for a fraction of a second. From the gaps issued a dim gold light. In the next instant it was gone, but it still drew Nathan's curiosity to the forefront – and completely overshadowed his attention to his enemy. The frog's metallic foot jammed itself into Nathan's vulnerable stomach and sent him into a tree.

For a minute there was hardly any air in Nathan's lungs, and they burned and shrieked at the emptiness. That shriek left him unable to even grunt at the rest of the pain searing through his body. All he could do was writhe as he searched for the strength to stand.

The frog made like it was casually checking its nails for dirt. It said, "I'll tell ya, though, I kinda wish you were a little better. But it was obvious 'Catholic School Girl' was just feeling the effects of my baby brethren."

Nathan finally reached his feet, and his spear was demoted to a walking stick to which he clung for dear life. The frog was hardly perturbed, and in fact it seemed to have grown bored.

"Hmm, I guess if I eat the girl, I'd be killing my baby brethren." It paused a moment in half-interested thought. "Does that make it an abortion?"

A wind of pure fury flowed through Nathan's body, thrilling him with newfound power. He readied his lance, took aim at the creature's head, and charged.

A rock suddenly hit him in the chest.

Wait, that ain't a rock, he thought. *And why did I stop?*

The tongue he'd thus far managed to dodge had lodged itself right in his heart. With a wet smack and a whoosh of air, it returned to its home in the monster's mouth. The homunculus purred at the taste of Nathan's blood. It gazed down at the body of its opponent, unceremoniously crumpled on the ground.

"You know what happens to a human when his heart is ripped out?" asked the beast. Then it hefted the inert spear into the air and gazed at its metal shimmering in the moonlight. "I get his spear, that's what!"

The frog laughed to itself a little longer, and twirled the spear in its hands. Then, as the elation of victory subsided – it wasn't much, really, considering how much of a pushover the schoolkid was – the frog grew a little dumbfounded.

"How do I revert this to a Kakugane?" he mumbled.

* * *

A dull, faded image entered Nathan's mind, tinted sepia like an old movie playing on a reel of worn-out celluloid. It elicited the same kind of feeling as when the history teacher forced them to watch old wartime videos. For a moment, it was like the silent ones, where there were explosions going off, but no sound.

The contents of the movie were not explosions, but things very much similar in the mind of a five-year-old child.

A little brunette girl sat in a heap on the concrete, clutching her head and screaming. Still no sound, which made it all the more haunting. A woman appeared from right field, embraced the little girl, and shot the camera a deathly glare. As the woman, who was undoubtedly the girl's mother, picked her up and took her inside for an icepack, another figure entered the view. This was a man, enormous compared to the person holding the camera. His head seemed to touch the sky as he thrust his finger at the camera. The mouth was moving, but there was still no sound.

Suddenly, it looked like it was raining on the lens, and then the view flashed dark erratically. A pair of dirty forearms wiped the lens dry, but the rain kept coming. It wasn't so blurry that Nathan couldn't see what those hands were holding as they tried in vain to rub the water out of the camera.

A cricket ball?

It was one of those hard leather ones, like the ones they use in professional games. He could remember playing with one of those, a long time ago. But something bad happened, which made his parents really mad. When they got back from the hospital with Ariadne, they banned him from TV, game consoles, and going outside.

He never played cricket again.

* * *

The gravel felt like a bed of needles against Nathan's cheek as he came to. He took a moment to assess himself: difficulty breathing, lightheaded-ness, and a hole in his chest.

A normal Friday night, he thought. *God I hope not!*

Something tickled at his outstretched hand that lay just within his dazed gaze. His eyeballs shifted to see the red sash of his spear resting softly on his hands.

My weapon. My new life.

He felt life in his fingers as they tangled themselves in the fabric. The threads hummed softly with an internal light as he gripped it. With his free hand, he pushed himself from the ground. Blood dribbled from his mouth and his chest as he ascended, but though he stood in a pool of the red life, he held himself up by sheer willpower.

The frog was walking away when it felt the spear pull backward. It turned to see Nathan still standing, the hole in his chest very much see-through. For the first time, the frog was confused and a little afraid. Not just because the boy was still standing with empty space where his heart should be; not just because the sash that connected him to the lance was shimmering with intensifying light; not just because the frog felt its stamina wane with the growing glow – though all of that was bemusing and plenty scary.

It was the face the boy wore. Blood trickled from his nose and mouth, his cheeks were battered and bruised, and his eyes radiated a force of determination and resolve.

With a deft flick of his wrist, the spear leapt out of the

frog's hands and toward Nathan. The boy charged forward, and caught the lance in time to deliver two swift slashes to the creature. Its legs and arms disappeared. Before it fell to the ground, Nathan gave a roundhouse kick that sent the dismembered body into a tree.

The frog gave an anguished growl as it hit the ground with a crash. Lacking arms, all it could do was flail in an attempt to crawl away. From its gaping wounds, mechanisms writhed like a colony of metal worms, wriggling about to seal the wound and replace the lost limbs. Nathan marched over the disintegrating body parts, the internals of his spear shimmering through the seams in its hull, and gazed down with a look to frighten the devil himself.

The frog wailed, "You have no heart!"

Nathan brandished his golden spear. "This is my heart! A new life, given to me by Astrid Rachelle. Try and take it, and you'll get curb-stomped!"

The frog proceeded to fret and thrash like a fish out of water, red tears trickling from its eyes as it cried, "What are you?"

The lance pointed downward, straight at the frog's face, and its wielder growled, "I'm the lightning, *toad*."

The wretch's final shriek devolved into a strangled gurgle, followed by a sickening crash of failing metal and squishing entrails, as the lance found its way home.

Nathan stood back, wheezing and drained, as the thing slowly disintegrated in the wind. A part of his mind wondered if he should be panting so hard given what was wafting into the air around him, but the rest of it was blank. He grabbed the lance, and it dematerialised into his chest. His body tingled as the wounds healed around him, but it drained him even more and he fainted.

Heretofore, an entity had watched from the safety of the bushes, concealed in darkness. That entity detached from the ground in which it had planted itself, and began to walk on its metallic roots. The roots and tendrils steadily melded together, and where they melded, they secreted dark brown

ooze that solidified into skin to mask the creature. Had
people been watching from the bridge above, they'd have
seen a naked woman standing over an unconscious boy. Her
dark complexion was smattered with hideous tattoos of
demonic plants, her spiked hair a bright pink. Her eyes
glistened yellow as she regarded Nathan with intrigue and
hunger.

*Part of me wants to devour it, the other … To fight even one of the
warriors that Burrumering spoke of.*

She knelt over the body and her long fingers grew even
longer as they caressed the boy's hair.

"Paddock was a weakling toad," she intoned. "Maybe
you should live a while longer, and fight me instead." Her
skin quivered, making the Venus flytrap tattooed across her
navel contort hungrily. "On the other hand, I've not had a
satisfying meal in ages."

The tendrils that were her fingers sprouted thorns that
locked into her prey. Then her jaw dislocated from her skull,
and an inner jaw protruded from within her throat. Those
mandibles, composed of thorned petals and oozing
steaming acid, eagerly advanced upon her prey.

"Homunculus!" bellowed a hated voice. The she-triffid
turned to the source of the noise, and saw the girl in the
Catholic uniform. Her thorns withdrew only slightly at the
sight, and she stood to face the girl who marched toward
her.

"The girl who has killed so much of my brethren,"
uttered the homunculus, her rose-petal mandibles ruffling
at the thought. She eyed the girl's limp, and intoned, "The
embryo nears your brain. Soon you will replace the brethren
you have slaughtered."

Astrid growled through gritted teeth, partly in an attempt
to intimidate her opponent. She tried very hard not to grip
the welt that latched to her stomach.

"It must feel strange," the homunculus went on. "When
I took this host, I met the brain immediately. And when I
touched this woman …" She ran her thorny tendrils over

the tattooed skin that was little more than a husk. "When I entered the world through her, I felt *alive!* But it was so quick; I hardly had a chance to know her truly ... Unlike you. That child has taken time to know you, to feel you," she lasciviously bit her lower lip, "To *touch* you."

With every word the beast uttered, Astrid's strength waned and she gripped her stomach. The embryo pulsated excitedly as if it knew one of its kindred was close. Her mental dam cracked, and she released a strangled gasp as she fell to her knees.

"Oh, look," cooed the homunculus. "It's kicking, isn't it?"

Astrid glared at the thing, and wanted to throw up, but still could not find the energy to speak.

"The way you clutch your belly," said the homunculus, her teeth glimmering as she smiled. "It's like you're pregnant ... Pregnant with my baby sister."

Astrid snapped. She drew her Kakugane and gripped it tightly.

"I'm no monster's mother!" she screamed. She raised the talisman, but the embryo didn't like that. Suddenly, it felt like her muscles were taken over by some unseen force, which held her arms down and kept her voice from working.

The embryo has hijacked my spine, thought Astrid as panic consumed her.

"You'll be a wonderful sister," said the homunculus with a joyous, encouraging tone. "Together, we'll feast!"

Feast! A festival. A school. Blood gushing like the rain rushing. Sharp teeth like an anglerfish, splitting the throat and bringing the finish. Mother!

Astrid screamed as a fiery rage electrified her nerves. The ravine lit up like a supernova, with her at the epicentre. When the light cleared, there she stood, her robotic arms glimmering triumphantly in the moonlight.

"Sorry, but dinner's cancelled!" she bellowed. The blades whipped into action, and slashed and swatted away the vines that issued from the homunculus' mouth and hands. The creature reverted to its true form, and its many tentacles and tendrils sought out the girl. Unfortunately for the creature, a fury-fuelled Astrid was too fast and strong. Her scythes hacked away at the humanoid plant with reckless abandon, her every slash punctuated by her screeches, until she found the being's flowering core. Wordlessly, she turned into a human buzz saw and shredded the monster, until it was dust.

Astrid's Arms Alchemy disappeared in a flash of light, and she fell to her knees. Sweat poured down her brow and fell onto her thighs as she sat, doubled over in agony. She took a moment, gathering what little lucidity she had left, and slowed her breathing.

In through the nose. Hold ten. Now release through the mouth.

A few repetitions later, her heart slowed and the pain subsided. The creature in her stomach continued to shudder, as if sobbing over the loss of two of its kindred. Astrid looked down at it with scorn and growled, "Complain all you want, you son of a bitch."

Oh, God, I'm already talking like him, she thought with a scoff.

Her strength returned, Astrid rose to her feet and gazed over at Nathan. He lay facedown, still unconscious but alive. The marks left by the homunculus visibly healed, but he would still need more treatment. She turned him over and glared at him.

"When you wake up, you'll wish you'd never been born," she said sternly.

Another entity watched from the shadows. This one held two plastic bags, one containing a lewd magazine and the other his best friend's sport tracksuit.

"What the fuck?" Klein intoned.

5 | Just an ordinary kid

"Murder the frog!" screeched Nathan as he sat up in a delirium. His chest tingled with rawness, and the itch of the bandages around his wounds only exacerbated his agitated nerves. The bed looked like it had only just been made before he was laid on it, and next to it was a small suitcase, hardly bigger than a laptop bag. The contents were visible between the seams of the haphazardly closed lid, and Nathan's cheeks turned red at what he could see within.

"Girl's undies," he murmured. He looked down and found himself wearing nothing but his own underwear, his own ruined and bloodstained uniform hanging from a hook on the wall nearby. He clutched the blanket close to his chest and looked around warily, gauging his situation.

What happened last night? I remember killing that frog, and then ... Nothing.

Then it struck him.

In a hotel room, in my undies, with a girl's suitcase nearby ... That must mean ...

He grabbed his hair in frustration, and squalled, "Gah! I had my first time, and I can't even remember it!"

Astrid exited the bathroom in light brown shorts and a green tee-shirt. She stopped towelling her hair dry at the sight of the livid boy bashing his head against a pillow.

"Nathan! What's the matter?" Astrid exclaimed.

Nathan turned and saw her, fresh out of the shower, and his face twisted into a mortified expression.

"It was with you?" he mumbled.

"Was what with me?" returned Astrid.

Nathan bolted off the bed toward her, and exclaimed, "My first time was with you?"

Astrid's eyeballs almost fell out of their sockets in shock. "What?"

Nathan had already jumped to his conclusion, and not even Astrid's bewildered and indignant expressions could budge him from it. One second he was laughing hysterically and the next he was on the verge of tears.

"I finally got some!" he exclaimed. "But I can't remember it," he lamented. "But it was with Astrid!" he cheered. "I hope I was good," he mumbled. He swivelled back to Astrid, who was still wide-eyed and wide-mouthed. "Hey, did I do good? Was I good to you? I can't remember, so …"

SLAP!

Nathan now had a dumbstruck face with a permanent handprint in the cheek.

"Are you awake yet?" asked Astrid.

"I may need another," replied the very embarrassed boy.

SLAP!

Ten minutes later, Nathan had showered and donned a clean set of clothes Astrid stole from his dorm room. He gingerly slurped the tea from the minibar, trying his best not to make eye contact with the girl.

Finally, he spoke up, "I'm sorry about earlier."

SLAP!

"What was *that* one for?" he exclaimed as he nursed his cheek.

"Taking on a homunculus alone," barked Astrid. "You could have died!"

"But I didn't," replied Nathan. "I kicked its arse. I was the lightning!"

"I found you nearly dead at the mercy of the rose-type,"

said Astrid. "If I had been slightly slower, you'd've been eaten."

Nathan's brain did a double take. "Rose-type? I didn't fight a rose-type. I think it was a frog." Astrid then shot him a confused glance. "Yeah, he was stalking you after we split up last night, and he was saying he wasn't going to let you become a homunculus. Instead, he wanted to eat you and take your Kakugane. So I fought him."

Astrid swallowed gauchely, "You should have called for me."

"Oh, yeah, I should have just asked the bloodthirsty creature, 'Sorry mate, could you wait a little bit while I call someone else over to kill ya?'" retorted Nathan.

Astrid pursed her lips and looked away, and Nathan could tell she knew she'd misunderstood the situation. She said, "Sorry then. I guess I should thank you, since you took on that monster for me."

"And I kicked its arse!" exclaimed the boy, punching the air above his head.

"Don't get too cocky," retorted Astrid. "I still had to save you from the rose-type."

Nathan downed the rest of his tea and slammed the cup on the table. "That means there's just the eagle, the lion, and Papillon."

"I'd say the lion is right here," said Astrid, pointing to her stomach. "Unless there's more cultures we didn't find in the lab, let's assume it's just Papillon and Burrumering."

Nathan nodded, and thought for a moment. Then he smacked his forehead in frustration, "Oh, damn it! I should have asked that frog before I killed him."

Astrid cocked her head slightly, "I figured I should have asked the rose woman too. I was in a bit of a mood though." She set her cup down and turned to Nathan. "It's not over yet. We looked through the whole of Year Twelve and couldn't find our guy. If he wasn't at school for a week, then the school would have an absence mark on the attendance record."

"Oh! So let's go check," said Nathan. Astrid reached into her suitcase, and procured a leather wallet concealing what was unmistakably an ASIO badge.

"Relax. It's a fake," she said. "The agency provides this to me when I need to pull rank."

Nathan could have cried tears of joy at how cool she was, but restrained himself to a wide smile.

"I'll check out the dorms," he said in a high-pitched voice that made Astrid sigh irritably. "The manager will have a record of people there, and I can ask around."

Settled on their plan, the pair donned their shoes and exited the hotel room. To Nathan's amazement, they were in the Novotel on North Beach. Astrid led him onto the shuttle bus, which took them along the route into the middle of the city. Nathan sat there, perturbed by the setting. Here he was, a boy with a magical spear, with a girl who had four robotic arms, riding the bus to get around.

Deadpool comes to mind, he thought.

He said aloud, "I'm a little surprised you were living in a hotel room all this time. And you're taking the bus, too."

Astrid shot him a confused look, "Where else would I be? Living in the sky, feeding off dew drops?"

"Or homeless," Nathan retorted with a sly grin. That earned him a solid shove from the girl.

"You shouldn't make assumptions about people you don't really know," said Astrid, shooting a scowl of half-serious offence.

Hmm, that's right, thought Nathan. *I don't really know much about Astrid, do I? We've either been looking for Papillon or training.*

"Well then, we've got time on the bus," he said. "What school do you go to?"

"It takes you a week to start asking?" returned Astrid with a smirk. "I don't go to school. The uniform I wear is from a girl's school I infiltrated on my previous mission."

"Oh, so you're a working girl," said Nathan. "So, umm … How old are you?"

"I turned seventeen six months ago."

Nathan whistled, "So you're older than me. I'll hit that mark about seven … eight months down the track." He scratched his head gauchely, and didn't notice Astrid's subtle smile as she glanced out the window. Another thought occurred to him. "So, this agency you work for," he muttered. "You guys have cool code names?"

Astrid sighed.

"Yes," she replied reluctantly.

"Awesome!" chirped Nathan. "What's yours?"

Astrid took some more coaxing before she replied, "Spartan Valkyrie." She expected him to swoon and marvel at how cool it sounded. Instead, Nathan just returned a confused look.

"That sounds like a stripper name," he said.

Astrid's jaw dropped and she punched him. She got him a few more times and he withdrew chuckling from her.

"Now that's just rude," she snarled.

Nathan sobered as Astrid held back her punches, though she continued to shoot him light-hearted evils.

"Seriously though, how did you get into this job?" Nathan asked.

Astrid's face turned dark and she looked out the window. Nathan asked again, but she didn't respond, and he grew concerned. He moved to ask her if she was alright, but noticed the white knuckles of her tightly clenched fists.

Touchy subject … None of my business, he concluded.

"Hey, we're at the bus stop," he said, grateful that the mood didn't last long enough to become too uncomfortable.

Astrid promptly headed up the road to the school, giving Nathan little more than, "I'll call you if I find something."

He marched toward the dormitories. It was late morning, and there was still a slow trickle of students leading out of the building and into town. Many of them were headed for the mall, while others were off to sport or drama clubs. Nathan regarded the crowd, recognising several of them. He wondered silently whether any of them knew any of Papillon's victims. The thought depressed him, and he internally vowed, *I will save these kids.*

He asked a few passers-by where the manager was, and they directed him toward the cafeteria. He went there, and looked around.

Not here, he thought. *The only time I want to see the rat, and I can't find him.*

Suddenly, a pair of hands grabbed him by the scruff of the neck and dragged him to his knees.

"Where the hell were you last night?" shouted Ariadne, seedlings of a tear in her eyes.

Nathan tried to pull away from his pale-faced sister, but either she'd been working out a lot in the last week, or she was so full of adrenaline that she'd attained super-strength. He eventually gave a half-hearted response, "I was with Astrid."

"Why didn't you answer my calls?" barked the distraught girl.

"Yeah, why didn't you?" asked Klein, who stood behind him, leaning against the doorframe with a pensive expression. Nathan was too busy with his sister's onslaught of slaps and shoves to notice the sheer distress that lay just beneath Klein's stoicism. Jessie or Paul didn't notice either as they walked up to ask, "We've been trying to call you. Didn't you bother to check your messages?"

Nathan patted down his pockets and exclaimed, "Agh! Crap! I must've left it at Astrid's hotel room!"

The words, *Astrid's hotel room*, not only brought an end to Ariadne's fretting; it also elicited the loudest hoot Nathan had ever heard. Jessie and Paul suddenly started patting him on the back and showering him with congratulations.

"So you and Astrid went and did it, did ya?" asked Jessie.

Nathan's face burned, "No, no, nothing like that. I just stayed at her place for the night."

Ariadne gripped her head in flushed horror and veered away from the rabble of boys. "Oh God! I did not want to picture that!"

Nathan tried to deny the conclusion they'd jumped to, all the while Klein, who knew better, just kept silent and cross-armed. He eventually offered a harrumph and approached his friend.

"Klein, I'd have thought you'd be first in line to pat him on the back," said Paul with a smirk.

Klein shrugged, "Meh. It's nice to know all my hard work training him has paid off."

"Oh, training," scoffed Nathan. "Handing out condoms like you've got any experience? That ain't training. Plus, me and Astrid ain't like that."

Paul nodded with fake seriousness, "Yes, you're saving yourselves for marriage, aren't you?"

Nathan gave a big holler to settle the rabble, and said, "Listen, I'm looking for the manager. Has anyone seen him?"

"Went into town for something," replied Ariadne. Her brother rolled his eyes and gave a frustrated sigh. At that, she asked, "Why?"

Nathan brushed them off and made a move to leave, but Klein stopped him.

"If you need help, maybe we can do something," he said.

Nathan swivelled around and regarded his friends, all of whom were confused and concerned. He recalled his earlier intention to spend last night with them – the night off Astrid gave him, which he couldn't enjoy on account of a certain British toad. An image of Ol' Chambo erupted into his mind, reminding him why he was so desperately trying to keep this secret from them.

But they might know what Papillon looks like, he thought.

Eventually, he said, "I'm looking for one of the Year Twelvers. He has something Astrid really needs, but we haven't been able to find him."

"What's his name?" asked Klein with a furrowed brow.

"Dunno," replied Nathan. "But I know what he looks like."

"Hey, if you know that, maybe I can do a sketch for ya,"

said Jessie. "Then we can all take a copy and go looking for him."

Nathan popped down with Jessie, who had grabbed a pencil and paper from his room. Half an hour later, and after several chats about the meaning of the words 'sharp jawline,' the drawing was finished.

"Behold! My masterpiece!" exclaimed Jessie, his blunted pencil held aloft like a sword. All that was missing was an epic round of Gregorian chanting to complete the image. The drawing was magnificent.

"Dude, since when can you draw like that?" asked an astounded Klein.

"Since always," replied Jessie. "I *am* doing art as an elective, you know? And I have a DeviantArt account as well. I keep trying to show you guys stuff but you're never listening."

"Freaking hell man, you should be more insistent!" exclaimed Nathan. He went to photocopy the drawing. By the time he was back, Ariadne was already begging Jessie for art lessons.

"Ok, you guys go and check around the dorm rooms," said Nathan, handing his friends a copy each. "Ariadne and I'll search the first floor. If you see this guy, *don't* – I mean it! – *Don't* talk to him. Give me a call and tell me where he is. Got it?"

"Yes sir," bellowed his friends, offering him a mock salute before setting off.

Nathan and Ariadne walked about the different common rooms, asking anyone they could find if they knew the person in the picture. Nathan even tried to describe the man in words, but only got blank faces in reply. After exhausting the entire first floor, they took to wandering outside the dormitory building. By then, Ariadne had lost interest in the search and her attention shifted to the drawing. She was so caught up in fantasies of being a great artist, she didn't realise she'd run into someone.

The boy was barely ten centimetres taller than her,

seemed very weak, and feebly tried to gather the paper bags he'd dropped. In a panic, Ariadne looked around for Nathan, who had vanished. She then bent over to help the boy with his paper bags.

"I'm so sorry," she said. "I wasn't paying attention. I didn't mean to knock you over."

She handed him the last bag and looked into his face for the first time. He looked like one of those really cute Asian boys. In her mind, he would have been a lot cuter if he didn't look so tired and dejected.

"It's quite alright," he said in a husky whisper. "I'm used to it."

Ariadne's tongue caught in her throat and she had no idea what to say next. Nathan appeared from behind her.

"Hey, Ariadne, I told you I was going to the loo, why didn't you wait?" he said.

"Sorry, I was looking at the drawing and I accidentally bumped into this guy," she motioned toward the boy, who had since silently walked away. They gave chase, and met with the boy near the water bubblers behind the building. He turned when they approached, and seemed quite surprised at their presence.

"Is there something I can do for you?" he stammered, a little taken aback.

"No, I just wanted to make sure you were alright," said Ariadne with a concerned smile.

"I'm alright," said the boy. He stole a glance at his bags on the concrete wall and murmured, "Could you give me a moment, please?"

He reached into the bags and pulled out a number of objects resembling flimsy ice-cube trays. Nathan took another look and realised they were the packs used by his grandparents to remember when to take what medications. Both his and Ariadne's eyebrows ascended their foreheads as more and more of the packs appeared. Then, the boy began opening the Saturday segment in each pack and emptying them into his mouth, one by one, followed by a stiff drink of water from the bubbler. When he was done, he bent over, his hands gripping the side of the bubblers for support.

"Whoa, that's a lot of pills, mate," said Nathan.

"Are you sick or something?" asked Ariadne.

"Something, I guess," panted the boy. "Now, you were going to ask something?"

"Oh yeah, we're looking for someone in Year Twelve," said Nathan. "I don't know his name, but we've got a sketch of him."

Ariadne slapped her head, "Agh! I left the sketch inside." She raced back into the building.

Nathan shook his head incredulously and murmured, "That girl'd forget her own head if it wasn't screwed on." He eyed the boy, who still breathed deeply as if his lungs weren't working as well as they should. Curiously, he approached the boy, who was quite a bit shorter than he, and asked, "Haven't seen you around here, mate. Are you new?"

The boy huffed silently and smiled, "No, I've been here a while."

Nathan held his hand out, "Nathan Grant. That silly twit is my sister, Ariadne."

The boy took it, the coldness of his thin fingers surprising Nathan as he said, "Koushaku Chouno. You can call me Chouno if you like."

"Sure, Chouno," said Nathan with a grin.

"Why are you looking for this Year Twelve student?" asked Chouno.

"He's got something that a friend of mine really needs," said Nathan, hoping that Chouno would be as interested as anyone else in his agenda. But this guy was clearly a lot more intrigued than most others in the dormitory.

"And I take it none of the other students know him?" he asked. Nathan shook his head. "He must be invisible, then. You know how that can be? He's a phantom. People see him in class, but nobody notices him."

Nathan gave him a one-sided smile, and muttered, "What? Like an undercover agent?"

"More like a piece of furniture," replied Chouno.

"Oh, so he's like a *Transformer*, hiding in plain sight," exclaimed Nathan, palming his fist. Chouno glared at him incredulously, but didn't get a chance to ask the boy if he was serious. Ariadne appeared with the drawing in hand.

"This is a picture of the guy we're after," she said as she handed it to Chouno. As he gazed upon the sketch, his face contorted into a delighted, almost aroused leer.

"Like the drawing, do ya?" asked Nathan upon noticing the boy's expression.

"It is a good drawing, even if it's of a weirdo in a creepy mask," said Ariadne.

"It's not creepy!" barked Chouno, before bursting into a coughing fit. When he recovered, he gazed longingly at the paper. Nathan opened his mouth to comment about the boy's lascivious expression, but when he saw those eyes, his heart almost stopped its subtle mechanical thumping. The boy's eyes grew transfixed and mesmerised by the mask, and billowed an air of psychosis.

The eyes you'd expect of a sociopath, Astrid's voice echoed in his mind.

"Ariadne, I think we'll go and get lunch," he said, trying to sound as nonchalant as humanly possible. Unfortunately, even a dimwit would have sensed the fear in his voice, as his eyes remained glued to the enraptured boy.

"What about the search?" asked Ariadne.

"We'll do it later," Nathan replied curtly. "I'm hungry. Go and get the guys together, and bring some of your friends. I'll shout you."

Ariadne's eyes darted between her brother and the boy. An itchy sensation of confusion tapped at the back of her mind as she took the picture from the boy and moved away. "Aren't you coming?" she asked over her shoulder.

"I'll meet you guys there in a minute," Nathan said, finally looking at her. He nodded her away, and then turned his eyes to Chouno. The boy rose to his full height, and he returned Nathan's glare with a gleeful grin.

Why did I forget my phone? Damn it, he cursed himself. He shook off his own nerves and steeled himself.

"Had to take a few sickies, Chouno?" he asked sternly. "Like a few days … A week, maybe?"

"What's it to you, Grant?" returned Chouno, his voice slightly deeper than before.

"Just wondering whether you've been putting it on," said Nathan, trying very hard not to touch his chest. "You know, so you can get time for your experiments?"

Chouno's smile widened.

"It's not like anyone would notice a *transformer* like me, hiding in plain sight," he grumbled. "I'm invisible, a piece of furniture, an unimportant caterpillar that wriggles in the mould." The boy reached into his jacket pocket and withdrew that all too familiar butterfly mask. When he set it upon his nose, his Asian-flavoured Aussie accent vanished, and the Italian accent Nathan knew well replaced it. "But now, that caterpillar has found the cocoon of Alchemy, and soon he shall be a butterfly."

Nathan grit his teeth, "You're the creator of the homunculi, Papillon!"

"Tsk, tsk!" Papillon waved his forefinger disapprovingly. "Pa-pi-yon! And put more *love* into it!" He took the stance of a ballerino on stage, as if a raucous applause filled his ears.

Nathan's body trembled with both fear and anger, greater than when he fought the frog.

This is the creator, the big boss, he thought. *He'll probably have a lot more up his sleeve than those guys did. I can't wait for Astrid. I gotta fight!*

His hand flew to his chest.

"Stop right there!" exclaimed Papillon, a green pill held in his outstretched hand. Nathan froze. "This is the antidote for your friend's homunculus embryo. I made it just in case I made a mistake in my experiments … I believe you jocks call it a *just-in-case.* But since I've finished my experiments, I don't need this anymore." Nathan made an advance toward Papillon, who withdrew his hand cautiously. "Oh, no you don't. *Quid pro quo,* Mister Grant. I haven't had a chance to fiddle with Arms Alchemy yet, but it is quite interesting. So, give me your Kakugane."

"Not a chance," snapped Nathan.

"Oh, so you don't care about your friend?" asked Papillon. He held the pill over the basin. "Well then, I'll just toss this down the drain."

"No!" cried Nathan. "I need that."

"I want your Kakugane," replied Papillon. "Either I get one now, or in two days when your friend becomes a homunculus." His vindictive grin widened and he enunciated, "So... what to do? What to do?"

"The Kakugane is part of me," replied Nathan. Papillon cocked his head. "I was killed by one of your homunculi. It ripped my heart out. Astrid saved me by implanting a Kakugane in my chest." He pounded his chest fervently. "This is the new life she gave me, and I couldn't hand it over if I wanted to."

Rather than being moved by Nathan's resolve or the touching story, Papillon began to dribble. He leaned forward voraciously and panted, "A new life! The Kakugane has *that* kind of power?"

Nathan backed away, anticipating an attack of unstoppable magnitude at any moment. Papillon's drool turned red as his bloodshot eyes glimmered with an opportunistic glow.

"Give it to me! Give me the Kakugane! Give me new life!" he bellowed as he advanced on Nathan.

An image of a cricket ball flashed through Nathan's mind, and in a fit of bewildered ire and involuntary strength, his fist flew into frail flesh. He didn't dare open his eyes. His whole body trembled like a hard-struck tuning fork. Suddenly, he felt a hand on his outstretched arm, and his eyes flew open to see Astrid, trying to calm him down.

He pointed out Chouno. The boy lay on the ground, out-cold, a long trail of blood flowing from his broken nose.

"He's got the antidote in his hand," he stammered. Astrid prised the hand open, and gave a partly disappointed look as she flicked the pill away.

"It's a fake," she said. "The real antidote is an injection." Nathan's jaw dropped and he felt a sudden urge to kick the boy while he was down. Astrid went on, "But we've finally caught the creator. Good job."

Nathan, having relaxed enough to think coherently, scratched his head and said, "Doesn't feel like a good job. I was expecting something a little more imposing for the boss of the monsters."

"Now who's the one who watches too many movies?" said Astrid with a smirk. "Though he has the knowledge and resources to create homunculi, take all that away and he's just an ordinary kid."

A voice trickled upward from the heap on the ground, and it growled, "I'm hardly ordinary."

6 | The Caterpillar in the Mould

The room seemed little different from that of any other boarder. A single bed occupied the wall beneath the window. The adjacent wall was home to a large whiteboard full of equations. The opposite wall hosted a desk and a set of shelves stuffed with textbooks on subjects such as Quantum Theory, Molecular Biology, and Psychology.

Not surprising, since these are fundamental to the principles of Alchemy, thought Astrid as she perused the bookshelf. She stole a glance to the unconscious boy on the bed, and wondered what other kinds of skills Chouno had. Then she looked back to the bookshelf. She knew something was odd about it, but she couldn't pin-point it as she stroked her chin. It didn't help that there was a steady stream of discomfort radiating through her body.

When it first struck her abdomen, the embryo felt like hot acid had been poured over her skin. That pain turned into agony as the homunculus slid its tendrils into her body, voraciously seeking out her brain. At least her immune system was slowing it, but she could feel its disgusting feelers crisscrossing their way up her spine like a marathon runner on the home stretch. That pain had now evened its way out across her entire torso, and dulled her senses. Those dulled senses, failing to see what she was certain was right in front of her, annoyed her even more.

Frustrated, she punched the bookshelf. The shelf depressed into the wall slightly. It switched on a light in her frustrated brain. She strutted out of the room, and checked the distance to the next room down. She even stuck her nose in the neighbour's room to gauge the distance to the wall the two rooms shared, ignoring the two students whose intimate moment she'd interrupted.

There's a space inside this wall, she realised. She went back to Chouno's room, yanked the shelf aside to reveal the hole in the wall just large enough for her to sneak through. What she found made her grit her teeth with fury.

Nathan burst through the door with an icepack. He roused Chouno, who begrudgingly took the cold bag and pressed it to his bruised face.

"I see you found my secret lair," he murmured through the icepack. Then Nathan noticed the hidden door. When he looked over Astrid's shoulder, he saw another forest of glass tubes and reaction chambers centred about a pear-shaped test tube. Another homunculus embryo pulsated within the glass womb.

Nathan glared at Chouno. "You son of a bitch! You lied to me."

"I told you I finished all my experiments," replied Chouno with a grin.

"You're going to kill someone else with this thing? Isn't it enough that teachers and kids have been murdered for your own sick hobby?" Nathan snapped.

Chouno turned to Astrid and uttered, "Your boyfriend is an idiot, I must say. This is hardly a hobby, you fool. This is my *life*."

"Start talking, Papillon," said Astrid. "How did you learn about Alchemy?"

"My great-great-grandfather left behind a compendium of his Alchemic research," said Chouno. His grin was saturated with pride as he continued, "Much of it was incomplete, and most of it was wrong anyway. But it was a necessary starting point, and I reinvented most of it on my

own. I suppose the teachers at school were wrong about me
… But then again, even *I* underestimate how smart I am."

"For what? Why create the homunculi?" cried Nathan.
"Didn't you know they were killing people? Didn't you
know the people you used those embryos on were going to
die?"

Chouno chuckled, "Of course I did. I just failed to give
two hoots. Partly, I was just curious. Also, I heard about
Alchemic Warriors and the Kakugane from my
grandfather's research notes, and I decided I might need
some protection."

Nathan pointed at the secret door, "What's that one for
then?" Tears were very near to his eyes as visions of the
snake devouring his sister sprung to his mind. He thought
of the embryo invading his friend's body, and he blurted,
"What? You got Astrid, and that last one is for me?"

"I doubt that," murmured Astrid. "We only found
twenty samples, and so far they've all been accounted for
and dealt with." She marched over and began pulling back
Chouno's sleeves and shirt collar, ignoring his protests as
she searched. When she found her target, she showed it to
Nathan: a puncture point, nestled into the inner junction
opposite his elbow. Astrid glared at Chouno. "You cultured
your own cells, and grew that embryo from them."

Nathan's brow knitted and he scratched his head. "So,
what? He's gonna clone himself?"

"In a manner of speaking," returned Astrid through grit
teeth. "He's going to turn himself into a homunculus."

"What?" exclaimed Nathan. He eyed Chouno, who wore
a smile to put Tom Hiddleston to shame. "You're going to
use that thing on *yourself*? If you're gonna kill yourself,
there's gotta better ways to go."

Chouno's grin grew wider. "There's an exception to
every rule, Grant. I'm sure your soon-to-be-dead lover
knows what I'm talking about."

"A humanoid homunculus," replied Astrid. "A
homunculus pretty much has the consciousness of the

animal it came from. The human dies and the monster takes its memory. But a humanoid is different."

"Instead of dying, my mind will simply remain as it is," said Chouno, salivating as if he were talking about the world's best Christmas present. "I will discard my body and live as a superhuman ... A *choujin!*" He struck a triumphant pose that radiated his excitement, before his face suddenly twisted. In the next instant, his face was in a bowl beside his bed, unleashing a torrent of bloody vomit. Both Astrid and Nathan withdrew from the horrid smell of bile that wafted from the boy.

The retching finished, and the boy gingerly set the bowl down on the desk. He panted, his whole body trembling as he gripped his aching chest. It was a moment longer before Nathan found the presence of mind to say, "You want to be a superhuman just so you can have a better constitution or something?"

"This body isn't just weak, you idiot! It's dying!" barked Chouno, his voice leaving him in a sickening rasp. He calmed himself down and wiped his mouth with the back of his hand. He tried to rise to his full height, but his severe stomach cramps dragged his shoulders back to a slump. He gave a resigned sigh, and went on, "Leukaemia, MS, lupus, I've lost count of the number of diagnoses I've been given. I'll be twenty in a few months, but I've been held back in Year Twelve three times thanks to all my hospitalisations. You think you've got it bad, girl? The pain you feel from that embryo over the course of a week? Triple it, and extend it for *years!* And you at least know *why* you're in pain, and you know *how* to fix it! I'm dying, in excruciating pain, and nobody has a bloody clue why." His fury exacerbated the pain in his stomach and he doubled over with a grunt.

"I checked your records," said Astrid. "Until three years ago, you were the top of every class. You took extracurricular lessons in business management and advanced engineering. You were even offered competing scholarships for MIT, Harvard, *and* Oxford. No one seems to know why your grades and attendance suddenly dropped off. They'd sent you to counsellors, career advisors, and no one could get through to you. It just seemed you'd become a bludger. At first I thought it was because you had become an Alchemist and were busy with your experiments … I was almost right."

Chouno glared at her from his place on the floor. "So you understand why I want to become a *choujin*. I want to save my life."

A snake forced its way into Nathan's memory as he stared at Chouno, nearly crying. The snake said to him, "There's always one thing you humans don't want to do, but can't pass off onto someone else: Die."

A hundred angry voices and pointing fingers rose against him in his mind, accusing him and belittling him. Involuntarily, he wondered how many times he'd left other people to do things he didn't want to do, and how he'd made them feel. A hot, piercing feeling pervaded his head as if poisonous acid had been injected into his brain and was invading every corner of his mind. His teeth gritted tightly, and he blurted, "At the expense of everyone you killed? You killed Chambo, me, almost killed my sister, and so many students at this school! And if you do become a *chode-jin* – whatever the fuck that means – you'll become a man-eating monster. You'll just keep on killing people in order to live. How is that okay?"

"I want to live," retorted Chouno curtly. "I don't want to die, in pain and misery. Above all things I want to live and I don't care who I have to kill to do it. You, who got to come back to life without any problem or consequence whatsoever, don't get to tell me I don't have a right to save myself."

"You have no right to save yourself," barked Astrid. "You'll not live at the expense of another human being, you mass-murdering son of a bitch." She took her Kakugane from her pocket, and bellowed, "I'm going to end your last experiment."

"No!" screeched Chouno. "I'll swear not to eat humans! Just let me finish that experiment! That's *my* new life! Let me have it, please! Let me live!"

Astrid's brow furrowed with determination, as did Nathan's. She raised her Kakugane, while he pressed his palm to his chest.

"Arms –"

BOOM!

The outer wall of the room buckled and shattered, spewing knife-like shards of glass inward. Nathan threw his arms around Astrid and made his back a shield as a wing composed of black metallic feathers threw them aside. The smoke and dust cleared. Nathan winced from his ringing ears, but he took the tiniest comfort knowing Astrid was unhurt, if a tad annoyed. The pair launched to their feet and confronted the new arrival.

"Forgive my tardiness, master," murmured Burrumering, his deep voice erupting from his intimidating eagle form.

"Never mind, Burrumering," replied Chouno with a joyous smile. He leapt over the ruined partition into his secret lab and yanked the embryo from its housing. He hugged the thing like a newborn child.

"Chouno! Don't do it!" exclaimed Nathan.

"He won't use it yet," said Astrid. "That thing will still have a day or so before it's viable."

"And you have a day before you become my servant," spat Chouno.

The embryo in Astrid's stomach must have heard its master speak, and seemed to love what it heard. Astrid cringed in pain and her legs buckled.

Burrumering's beak glistened with his ire. In the next instant, Astrid and Nathan were squirming in his talons.

"Take them far away, Burrumering," bellowed Chouno. "Far away, and devour them. See to it they'll not interfere with my plans."

In an instant, the eagle vanished into the sky. Chouno

stood silently in the ruins of his home, and gazed at the dot that grew faint on the northeast horizon. As it flew over the escarpment and out of sight, he mumbled, "Why should you get to live so bloody easily, while I die, with no chance?"

His dorm room destroyed, he gave a disappointed huff before slipping out of the still intact door. Not a single student, or even the dormitory manager, who came to see what had happened, noticed the hunched Japanese boy skulking away. Whoever did see him assumed him little more than a friendless nerd carrying his latest science project.

7 | The Eagle Soars

Boarders returned from their Saturday outings to see a commotion in front of the dormitories. They all gasped in shock at the smoking hole in the roof. The dormitory manager, along with a team of nervous teachers, did their best to navigate the flurry of panicked students and perform a head count. But trying to keep order amidst a terrified group of teenagers was an insurmountable task – especially for a twelve year old looking for her brother.

"I can't find him," shrieked Ariadne. She tried to get the attention of the nearest teacher, who gave only a pre-programmed response of 'I'm looking right now' when she pleaded for help. Klein, Jessie, and Paul found her sobbing in the middle of the crowd and managed to bring her out of the way.

"Where's Nathan?" asked Klein.

"We were talking to one of the students, and he asked me to come and find you guys so we could go to lunch," said the distraught girl, though her voice was distorted by her ceaseless sobbing. "I was looking for you guys, but got distracted by something on TV. Then suddenly the whole building shakes and there's a big hole in the roof and I can't find Nathan!"

The girl broke down and buried her face in Klein's chest. He gave her an awkward pat on the back, which did nothing to stop her crying. He turned to his friends.

"You saw the thing on the roof, right?" he asked with a knowing glance.

"Looked to me like a big robot bird," replied Jessie.

Paul adjusted his glasses and intoned, "Nathan dreams up a girl with a Catholic uniform, then Astrid shows up in a Catholic uniform, then a robot bird trashes the dorms and Nathan goes missing. Coincidence?"

Klein pursed his lips and seriously considered telling them about the plant monster he watched Astrid fight the previous night. He wrestled with himself a moment, and tried to think of things they could do for their friend. On the other hand, if he did tell them, they might not believe him or even know what to do if they did believe him. Then he looked down at Ariadne, a trembling wreck missing her big bro.

You can't do anything for him, man, he told himself. *All you'd do is upset her.*

"Fuck!" he growled silently, cursing his powerlessness.

* * *

Burrumering's talons squeezed his prey so tightly their lungs had no room to expand. That and the low-pressure air rushing past their popping ears made for an excruciating flight that heretofore only very unlucky rodents experienced. Nathan could feel himself blacking out. He managed to open his lids a creep, the slipstream stinging his fast-drying eyes, and saw Astrid struggling. She looked back at him, and they nodded.

Astrid squeezed her Kakugane and shrieked, "Arms Alchemy!"

The mechanical scythes slashed at the underside of the eagle, not even denting it but distracting it enough to release its prey. Nathan waved his freed arms and unleashed his own spear. He gazed at Astrid, then at the ground that speed up to meet them. With what time Nathan had to gauge the high aerial view, he saw that Burrumering had carried them far away. Wollongong sat on the horizon to the far southeast, a small patch of whitish-grey between the ocean and the green escarpment. To the north was the bustling metropolis of Sydney. Below them was a carpet with trees and patches of open glades.

"Nathan," screamed Astrid, though her voice was barely audible over the screeching rush of air. She outstretched her hand and he caught it. Now that they were closer, her voice was more audible, but only barely.

"Having fun yet?" jibed Nathan.

"Do you have to ask?" retorted Astrid, looking downward. "I should be able to brace us." Her scythes pointed toward the ground, but they were trembling and rickety. Astrid grit her teeth tightly, and tried to focus her mind through the discomfort of the embryo stimulating her pain centres.

"Hang on, Astrid, I've got this," said Nathan. He pointed his spear downward. "Moonlander on Windows!" he said with a cocky smile that earned only a dismayed eye-roll from his skydiving companion. He focused his thoughts into the tip of the spear.

"Thruster!" he roared. The seams along the spear's surface erupted with golden light. A maelstrom of air and heat radiated downward like exhaust from a rocket nozzle. He kept his mind focused on the word *thruster.* Then his mind betrayed him.

Thrust her?

Blood filled his cheeks and threw off his concentration. His spear went haywire and threw them off balance. Golden tendrils of fire singed the air around him. Luckily, they weren't so far from the ground that Astrid couldn't recover. She stumbled on her landing, while Nathan landed face-first into the charred dirt.

"What happened?" barked Astrid.

"Sorry, I got distracted," replied Nathan as he rubbed his sore head. "But, hey! Didn't I stick that landing, eh?"

"Focus, you idiot."

Astrid pointed to the sky, from where their enemy nose-dove toward them. Nathan and Astrid huddled together, and thrust their weapons into the air to parry Burrumering's supersonic blow. The strength with which they held their ground surprised the beast, and he darted to the left to avoid their counterattack.

The beast hit the ground and transformed into a mechanical man. His wings were still there, their black finish glimmering in the mid-afternoon sun. The rest of his body was coated in yellow and black armour, which melded together organically as if it were skin.

Astrid glared at the beast, and Nathan wasn't sure if she was scared of the homunculus before them or the one inside her.

"Astrid, this guy has multiple homunculus forms," he murmured as the metal birdman approached them. As Burrumering spread his wings hostilely, he resembled a mechanical angel.

"He's not like any homunculus I've encountered," replied Astrid. She eyed the razor sharp claws he had for hands, and wondered how they'd compare to a bear's claw – not that she had any basis for comparison.

"I'm not like anything you've seen," bellowed Burrumering. "My master sure did see to it. I'll destroy you here, and then re-join my master as he completes his magnum opus."

Nathan grunted, and began twirling his spear in his hand.

"No one's getting destroyed except you," was what he started to say, but part way through he lost his grip on his spear and it fell to the grass beside him. His heart sank as he gazed around sheepishly.

"You won't beat me by trying to be cool," retorted Burrumering.

"My partner is an idiot," said Astrid apologetically. Nathan shot her an indignant look, and was going to retort before she added, "But don't underestimate him. Your frog brethren did that, and he met his end."

Burrumering swiftly closed the distance between them

to look Astrid dead in the eye.

"Do not compare me to that toad," he growled.

The swipe came faster than Astrid's eye could see. So did Nathan's spear. He parried Burrumering's blow, giving Astrid time to dart to the side and bring her blades over the beast's neck. His wings blocked the blow and threw her off in a single graceful move. Burrumering then turned to Nathan. He burst through the boy's feeble defences and delivered a kick to his stomach. The metal foot felt like a cannonball as Nathan flew through the air and landed at least thirty meters away. He felt on the verge of suffocating. He panted heavily and gathered his strength for another attack.

Astrid swung one of her scythe arms the left, another to throw off Burrumering's right flank, and brought the remaining two over his shoulders. Again, she hit the wings. A sudden feeling of ballistic weightlessness and a searing sting across her stomach and chest followed her frustration. She hit the ground and stained the grass with her blood, leaking from three long gashes leading up from her stomach to the middle of her chest.

"Fucking embryo slowing me down!" she screamed as her mechanical arms threw her to her feet.

"Foul mouthed and wild," intoned Burrumering as he gazed at the bloodied opponent before him. "Even when you become one of my brethren, you'll still be a danger to my master. I must deal with you quickly."

Astrid growled furiously at the continued mention of her turning. Her hair stood on end as if she were an arachnophobe with a thousand tarantulas crawling over her. The wretched creature wriggled and shrieked within her abdomen, and her wounds bled more. In her daze, she saw Nathan pull himself to his feet and charge. Using her mechanical arms to propel her, she launched herself at the creature.

Her blades hit the wings *again*. The monster's left hand grabbed her head and threw it into the ground. Then

Burrumering deflected Nathan's spear with his right, whipped around, and delivered a roundhouse kick that launched Nathan clear across the plain.

"You cannot sneak up on me, fool, even if you didn't breathe louder than a heaving boar," said the monster. "I sense your attacks in the wind before you even think to use them."

Burrumering gazed down at the pathetic writhing heap on the ground, and hefted her up by her head. Her scarred face contorted into an exhausted, resigned sneer. She tried to throw a punch, but he caught it with lightning speed, and twisted the arm to the side.

"I am not one for sadism," said the homunculus. "I'll make this quick."

"Nathan's coming for you," Astrid mumbled through the pain that had become a dull white noise in her head.

"I can sense him coming," replied Burrumering. "I shall send him soon after you."

"He's really fast, so you might not sense him," Astrid insisted. "Seriously, you'd best look, just in case."

Burrumering decided to humour his victim and glanced in the direction of the vanquished Nathan. Meanwhile, Astrid closed her eyes tightly to avoid being blinded by a devastating flash that struck Burrumering's eyes. When she heard his surprised growl, she took her chance and swung her blades with all the force she could muster.

A crash of torn metal echoed through the valley, followed by a stiff howl and a pitter-patter of feet sprinting across the grass. Burrumering crumpled to the ground, gripping a sparking gouge where his right shoulder used to be. The remains of his arm and wing lay in a mangled heap next to him, slowly disintegrating and wafting away in the wind. He glared at the floating flurry of evaporated metal, and for the first time in his life cursed the wind. Then his deep yellow eyes went outward to scan the terrain. Too bad that flash left his long-sight blurry. Though the pain was excruciating, he pulled himself to his feet and calmed his nerves.

Forget the wound, he thought. *When you feed, you will regenerate. You still have one wing. Focus on the wind. Focus on the hunt.*

* * *

Shouldering the wounded Astrid, Nathan hobbled through the trees. He took what little time he had to look over his shoulder to see if Burrumering was following. However, when he did so, he inevitably dragged Astrid around in a circle, and that wasn't helping the bleeding gashes along her torso.

"Rest here," Astrid gasped. "He'll take a bit to regenerate, and we'll be alright here." Nathan released her and she collapsed against a tree. Her metal arms vanished in a flash of light, the Kakugane reforming in her hand. She pressed it to her chest, and focused on steadying her breathing. Nathan stood wide-eyed as the wounds slowly sealed themselves. They didn't fully heal, and instead remained as a set of pink parallel lines in the twitching skin. The veins of the homunculus embryo were still visible through the tears in her bloodstained shirt.

"It's like you're Wolverine," Nathan mumbled.

"Yours is a lot more efficient, since it's part of your body now," replied Astrid breathlessly. She gazed down at the scars, and the pulsating embryo near them. "The wounds haven't healed fully though, thanks to this rotten bugger. Kakugane should be able to remove scars as well."

Nathan cocked his head, "What about the one across your face? Why doesn't it heal that?"

Astrid consciously placed her hand over her nose, as if to conceal a pimple.

"I choose to keep this one," she mumbled. "It was the first scar I obtained as an Alchemic Warrior."

Nathan wanted to press further, but recalled his friend's mood on the bus when he asked her why she fought the homunculi. He decided not to inquire further, and said, "It makes you look cool."

Astrid tried not to blush, but the fight did not go her way and she fumed. She glared at her friend and said, "You shouldn't be trying so hard to look cool! You tried to act like you're in a movie, and dropped your guard."

Nathan threw his hands up, "Hey, I'm sorry, okay? I won't do it again."

"Why do you bother with poses and all that?" she asked as she palmed her face.

Nathan shuffled a bit as he gave it some thought, then he said, "I guess it's to get me pumped. I figure if I take a cool pose, it'll boost my confidence and my attack's'll be more effective."

Astrid was about to retort, but her mind immediately went to the time they first fought Papillon. She recalled how she roared, and how it raised her resolve. Other times in her past came to mind, where a hefty screech amped her fighting instincts to victorious levels.

Her eyes darted aside and she murmured, "Makes sense, I guess."

"So, how are we gonna take care of Burrumering?" Nathan asked as he began twirling his spear around. Astrid didn't respond. Afraid he might be annoying her, he stopped playing around and looked at her. Her eyes were directed downward. Then she gazed at him.

"I've got a plan," she said.

* * *

Burrumering's beak-nose drew deep of the air, its cool flow ebbing away at the pain of missing a right arm. His only wing extended outward and let its metallic feathers hang loose in the breeze. His every receptor focused on the currents, sensing every tiny fluctuation in the air around him.

Instantly, he knew the life forms all about him.

A kookaburra nest in the trees to the north ... An ant colony to the south ... Cars on the freeway, heading down the mountain ... Must be home time for Sydney workers. Possums to the east. Good tucker until I find those warriors.

His true quarry was not to be found.

He paced, slightly unbalanced to his right side, his eyes glued to the ground in search of tracks. But he was a hunter of the skies, not a bloodhound. His senses of taste and smell were dull compared to his eyesight, and even then his eyes remained blurred from the flash of that boy's spear.

There is something else, he pondered as he recalled the boy. *I didn't sense his movements when he blocked my attack against the girl. And his wind … it is something I've not felt before. Hardly a breeze, but it forebodes a cyclone.*

He cleared another line of trees and entered a field further to the north. The gurgling chuckle of the kookaburras threw off his senses, like they always did when he hunted. He wished he still had his other wing so he could fly up and feast on the pests. The pain in his phantom limb spiked.

Don't be distracted! You must do well for master. For your loyalty!

The winds to the east ruffled his feathers, and Burrumering swivelled to see Nathan. His determined face fuelled that same anomalous turbulence that tickled at Burrumering's wings. The boy pointed his spear like a jousting lancer, and began to charge. The spear's red sash began to glimmer, and as the boy's roar grew in volume and fervour, so did the golden light grow in radiance.

Burrumering prepared his sole wing as a shield, and braced for the boy's impact. He returned the boy's glare with piqued interest.

It is only him, and his wind is still little more than a soft whisper of a gust.

The feathers twitched!

Wait! What's this new flow? This isn't the same as before!

Burrumering's eyes finally saw what his wings foretold, and Nathan could see it in his shocked expression. With a cry of "Shit!" he screeched to a stop, but the girl sprinting behind him did not. She leapt, using his shoulders for an extra boost, and soared toward Burrumering. He lost his focus a moment, long enough for Astrid to throw his wing-shield aside and deliver a series of slashes to his torso.

Infuriated, the beast swiped the girl away with his wing. He moved on her but had to dart backward to avoid Nathan's charge. He only just managed to deflect the spear, though it gave Astrid further ground to press her attack. She threw swipe after swipe with her mechanical arms, which made several persistent dents against his wing. He relaxed a little when his feathers ruffled with news of her dwindling strength. When it dropped enough, the wing flexed and threw her off balance. Then the sole of his foot embedded itself in her chest and launched her across the field.

Astrid desperately tried to scramble to her feet. At first, her legs moved, then they felt tingly, and then nothing. Paralysed from the waist down, she fell into a panic as the homunculus charged her, his claws ready for the final blow. She desperately crossed her arms and blades in front of her to shield herself, and heard a clang of metal on metal. Her eyes opened, and saw Nathan's back as he wrestled with the beast.

"Astrid! What's the matter?" he grunted as he pushed back against Burrumering.

"My legs are numb! They won't move!" shouted Astrid.

"The embryo's in her spine," said Burrumering, though he actually appeared more concerned than elated. He eyed Astrid, then Nathan. The soft wind was still there, and he could not help but be curious. His strength waned slightly, giving Nathan an opening to push back and swipe at him. Burrumering raised his wing-shield again, and endured the thrashing Nathan brought down upon it. The boy foolishly brought a blow to the right, mistaking the lack of a right arm for an opening. Burrumering deflected the stab with his wing, swivelled and punched the boy aside before charging at the immobile Astrid again.

Once again, he hit Nathan's spear.

How is he moving so fast? I didn't sense him that time, either.

What is it about this boy? Is it strength? Typical human hubris? Or perhaps the girl?

"Boy, why do you defend this girl so?" asked the beast. "Is she your lover?"

Nathan faltered slightly, and Astrid would have knocked his block off for it, were she able. Luckily, Burrumering's curiosity overrode his interest in the fight and he didn't exploit the opening.

"Don't get distracted by him, you bloody idiot!" barked Astrid.

"Well, you're not really my lover, are you? We don't want people getting the wrong idea," replied Nathan.

"Who cares if *he* gets the wrong idea!" screamed Astrid.

Burrumering backed away and said, "I must know. Why do you fight for her?"

Nathan brandished his spear and said, "I was killed by one of your brethren. Astrid brought me back to life and gave me this spear. Why wouldn't I fight to defend her?"

Burrumering gasped, and Nathan shrewdly took the chance to strike. He almost had the beast, who raised his shield just in time. As he beat against the creature, he continued to yell, "And I have to defend my friends from your master, who made you monsters that eat people! How can I not defend them?"

Suddenly, the spear tip was in Burrumering's claw, and he gazed fixedly at Nathan.

"You and I are the same," he said. "Before I had this form, I was an eagle, the lord of the skies. I don't know whether it was by poachers or accident, but I was shot down. As I lay there, broken and ruined, and waiting for death in agony, my master appeared. He brought me back to life, and gave me this body. Now that he is in danger, how can *I* not defend *him*?"

Burrumering threw the spear aside, punched Nathan and kicked him through the air. The boy shot to his feet, his face tainted by indecision.

"We're nothing alike," he barked. "Astrid saved my life

because she wanted to. Chouno only brought you back as an experiment. He hides like a coomer while your brethren kill and eat other students. He runs screaming while you fight his battles. He's only trying to save his own sorry arse!"

Burrumering retorted, "Same as any other animal. Whether you are a cowering possum or a soaring eagle, all creatures fear death and do what they can to avoid it. Animals eat other animals to survive. Even plants may eat other plants. Typical humans, thinking yourselves above nature, branding as enemy what's above you in the food chain! My master is only trying to live, as we all are."

"We're not the same," screamed Nathan, slashing blindly. Astrid wanted to call out to him, tell him to calm down and regain his footing. But she was too mesmerised by the battle of words going between them, and too outraged by the rationalisations Burrumering was shovelling.

Burrumering threw Nathan off again, and gazed at the boy who once again dragged himself to his feet.

"It's not cowardly to fear death," he intoned, recalling all the screeching rabbits, wailing wallabies, and fidgeting possums he'd consumed over his two lifetimes. "It's not shameful to run from it either."

Nathan glared at Burrumering, and saw his solemn expression. He took from it a tiny seedling of meaning, which elicited the kind of thoughts that all humans in the modern world have at one time or another, but few dare to consider. He could not help but wonder what he would be willing to do, if he faced the kind of fear that Burrumering had faced.

But I have, haven't I?

"I know how terrifying it is," he grumbled. "I've died, you've died, so we both know how scary it is, and how much it canes. But you know that it canes a hell of a lot more to be the one that gets to live, don't ya? Chouno and I are still human. And since you were once also a human, you'd know this too: there are things we must never do, even if it means death!" Nathan readied his lance, and the sash lit up brighter than the sun. "And there are things we have to do, even if it kills us!"

Every fibre of Burrumering's being trembled with elation and terror, and goosebumps erupted across his metallic hide as Nathan charged. That tiny breeze evolved into a maelstrom about the beast, and it tore the feathers from his wings, the armour from his body, and the breath from his lungs. As the lance passed through his prone body, though the pain was more excruciating than any gunshot, he felt the most perfect sensation of ecstasy, as if a salve had been placed over a wound he didn't realise marred his soul. As the flash cleared, a steady cloud of black and gold metal wafted upwards from the heap on the grass.

"Your wind is of a different kind, Nathan Grant," murmured Burrumering. "Know this, that wind will carry you to high and far places, and you mightn't like where you land. Be prepared."

Nathan stood over the felled beast, panting as he replied, "I'll be ready for what this world throws at me."

Burrumering smiled, and pleaded, "Don't kill my master."

"Never intended to, mate," said Nathan.

Though it was his last moments, Burrumering could not help but chuckle, "Never been called 'mate' before. Perhaps this world is not as dark, or hostile, as my master thinks … As I once thought."

Then he was gone.

* * *

The sun had long set below the horizon before Nathan woke from his snooze. His joints still ached, and the heavy bruises across his stomach from Burrumering's beating still stung when he moved. The soreness when he inhaled told him at least one rib was broken. His metal heart still clanged in his chest, and chugged away to heal his wounds.

"The Kakugane doesn't work as well when you're out of

stamina," said Astrid, her eyes fixed to the sky.

Nathan sat up from their place in the grass and looked down at her. The setting and time made for a scene from a romance novel.

A good one … One not written by Stephanie Meyer, thought Nathan. *Too bad Astrid's not my girlfriend … Oh, and the embryo still eating away her insides.*

"Feel well enough to walk yet?" he asked.

"Still paralysed," said Astrid as she tried to wiggle her unresponsive toes. "My arms are feeling a little heavy now." They both gazed dejectedly at the shattered remains of her mobile phone, which must have been destroyed during the battle.

"If only I hadn't left mine in your hotel room," said Nathan. "We could call an ambulance, or at least one of your buddies." He huffed, and looked around the field. When he saw nothing of note, he found himself looking up and down Astrid's prone form instead. Though it was a hell of a lot more interesting than grass, he had to keep himself focused. He pulled himself to his feet and slapped his legs to wake them up. Then he reached down to Astrid. "Shall we get going?"

"No," replied Astrid. "I'm not going. You are."

"Bollocks to that, girl," retorted Nathan. "You're coming with me if I have to drag you."

Astrid glared at him and barked, "I'm not a damsel in distress, Nathan. You won't gain anything from saving me. I'd say I've got twenty-eight hours before this thing reaches my brain. Based on where we are, I'd say it'd take you at least a day to carry me back to Wollongong, even if we left now. And then you'll have to find Papillon and get the antidote. I'll be a homunculus before you can find him."

"I'll just sprint then," replied Nathan.

"And hurt yourself even more?" shouted Astrid.

With a furious growl, Nathan started frantically pacing around her. His face grew hot with frustration and anger at the thought of leaving his saviour to die alone.

"You saved me," he said. "After I screwed up and died for nothing. Now I have a chance to actually return that favour, and you won't let me?"

"I'm not going to let you waste your time and energy to carry me back to civilisation, where all I'll do is rampage and kill your friends and sister," retorted Astrid, her voice calm and controlled like a soldier ready to swallow the little red pill. Though she spoke about her own impending death, she was far less emotional than the boy who scoffed and tried to yell her into submission. "I'm out of time. I was out of time before we killed Burrumering. That's why I leapt over you before. I figured I could at least help you beat him. And now, *you* have to finish what I started here."

Nathan's brow furrowed and he fell silent. Astrid reached into her pocket and handed him a folded piece of paper, crinkled from the afternoon's action.

"I found the address of a house belonging to Chouno's family in his student file," said Astrid. "You go there, and prevent him from using that last embryo. And if you can't stop him becoming a homunculus, you'll have to kill him." She grabbed him by the scruff of the neck and looked fixedly into his eyes, "Steel your resolve, Alchemic Warrior, and end this fight."

Nathan broke out in goosebumps at the girl's words.

Goddamnit! Even when she's dying she's still cool!

"Once it's over, another man will show up … My superior. You'll know who he is. Tell him everything," Astrid went on. "Then, please, go back to your life with your friends and sister."

The boy gazed back at her longingly, his brow knitted with impending remorse and regret. He fought back his tears with a sniff.

"And what about you?" he asked shakily.

Astrid smiled, satisfied that she'd convinced him, and laid her head back.

"Well, if you'd stay with me a little longer," she began. "I'd like to enjoy the stars a while before I get you to …

You know … Help me."

Nathan tried not to gnash his teeth with anger at what his friend and saviour had just asked him to do. It was obvious from the tightening of his jaw and neck he really didn't like the idea. Astrid kept her eyes fixed on him, boring a hole into his head that carried her demand as if it were an order he could not disobey. He eventually huffed acquiescently and lay down beside her.

"We'll watch the stars a little longer, okay," he muttered through clenched teeth.

"Thanks," replied Astrid with a smile.

"Then I'll go," said Nathan.

"Sounds good," intoned Astrid.

"Carrying you," Nathan promptly blurted.

"Yep …" Astrid's mind did a mortified double-take. "Wait! What?"

Her gaze met Nathan's mischievous expression, and her heart sank.

"You said 'yep' to me carrying you, so let's go!" bellowed a grinning Nathan. He swatted her protesting hands out of the way and hoisted her onto his shoulders. She screeched and wailed furiously as Nathan began to jog across the dimly moon-lit prairie, carrying her piggyback-style.

"Put me down, you retard," screamed Astrid. "I gave you an order to leave me there! If you try to run home carrying me, you'll collapse from exhaustion before you get down Mount Ousley!"

"Oh, please! Running around the world is like a morning jog for me," returned Nathan, that same dopey smile of triumph plastered over his face.

"Not carrying me!" retorted Astrid.

"Come on, it's not like you're Jabba the Hutt," replied Nathan. "At the very most, you're Fat Bastard."

"Stop trying to be cool and put me down!" barked Astrid.

"Nope!"

"Put-me-down, *NOW!*"

"Never!"

"Please put me down!"

"Impossible!"

Astrid gave up pleading long before they got within eyesight of the freeway.

8 | The Cricket Ball

Ariadne's eyes were sore from wiping away tears of worry. They were red and puffy, as if she'd been rubbing her face with poison ivy. Her school friends and one of the female teachers tried to comfort her as the police officer stepped away and pocketed his notebook. Another officer took statements from Klein, Jessie, and Paul, while another interviewed the manager.

The whole night had been a terrible worry for most of the boarders at the dormitory, all of whom were accounted for – except two. While most had never heard of Koushaku Chouno, whose dorm room had collapsed, they had all heard of Nathan Grant. The idiot hadn't answered his phone since he disappeared, right around the time the roof on the west wing of the dormitory building had collapsed. Though no bodies were found in the wreck, rumours disclosing the worst continued to run rampant. That did nothing but amplify Ariadne's worry, which continued all the way through the day until the cops were finally called in the late afternoon.

The police finished interviewing everyone concerned. The lead officer turned to Nathan's friends and said, "We'll put a missing persons note out to every unit and let you know. But if he turns up, give us a call."

"Will do, sir," replied Klein, shaking the officer's hand. They all walked out of the building to see the police off, and stopped flabbergasted at what they saw walking toward the front door.

"Hey guys!" Nathan called out breathily. He bent forward a little to balance Astrid's weight, which he bore piggyback-style. Astrid did everything she possibly could to hide her absolutely crimson face from the befuddled gawkers, but that only made it look like she was nuzzling closer to Nathan's neck. That wasn't the crowning feature of the whole picture. That prize went to Nathan's shirt, *on Astrid*. He was bare-chested like Tarzan, and covered in dirt and scratches.

Everyone went absolutely bananas. The crowd was alight with squeals and salacious hoots, which only made Astrid's cheeks burn brighter.

"Please, I'm begging you, just kill me," she droned.

"Can't," whispered Nathan, unable to hold back his grin through his exhaustion. "Cops are here, and I'd get put on trial for murder."

"I'll kill you, then kill myself," she murmured, though that was less due to the advancing homunculus embryo and more the humiliation she was enduring.

While the teachers tried to subdue the out-of-control rabble of teenagers, the police approached Nathan.

"Do you realise how much concern you've caused your friends and sister, Mister Grant?" asked the lead officer.

"Yes sir, and I'm really sorry for that," replied Nathan.

"Can you tell us your whereabouts yesterday and today?" asked the officer.

Nathan brought Astrid inside, and seated her on a couch in the common room, then turned to the cops.

"Sorry about that," he said. "My girlfriend here has a chronic slipped disc, and when it flares up she can't move. I'd gone to meet her, and while we were out, we slipped and fell down a hill near Heaslip Street. That's when the slipped disc flared up."

There were a number of rolled eyes and dismayed scoffs, and some even yelled, "You don't need to make up excuses.

If you were shagging, just admit it."

Nathan tried to ignore them, but the little voice in his head demanded that he grin at the idea. That then elicited many a homicidal thought in his so-called girlfriend's head.

"Why didn't you call for help?" asked the officer.

"Wanted to, but I'd left my phone at her place, and hers broke in the fall," said Nathan. "And I let her wear my shirt because hers got torn off in the fall too."

Astrid almost put her face through her palm as an absolutely scandalous hoot reverberated through the room. One of the cops started to shuffle irately, another grinned at the students' reactions, while the leader remained stoic. He turned to Astrid.

"Do you need a doctor, young lady?" he asked.

"No, I'll be alright," said Astrid curtly. "All I need is a proper night's rest on a proper bed, and I'll be fine."

She could read the cop's scepticism in his eyes, particularly when his gaze darted to where she subconsciously gripped the side of her stomach. He turned to Nathan, who wore a smile typical of a cartoon character trying to hide something behind his back. Eventually, the police officer huffed and said, "Well, it seems everything is alright. Be careful next time."

"Yes sir," said the couple in unison.

The officer glanced at Astrid and said, "You've got one hell of a boyfriend to carry you like that on his own. He's a real keeper."

The crowd simmered again with giggles and hoots, including a few who hummed the bridal waltz. Astrid's Arms Alchemy almost spontaneously formed when she heard that, but luckily the homunculus embryo kept that in check. The cops left and the crowd began to disperse. Before Nathan could turn to Astrid, a pair of fists jammed themselves in his still-tender gut. Ariadne glared at him with stinging red eyes.

"You left your phone at Astrid's place?" she screamed. She punched him harder and harder. "You arsehole! You shithead! You fucking –'' Nathan caught her arms and gagged her with his hand.

"Language, my dear sister," he scolded. "That's not the kind of talk fitting a twelve-year-old lady."

"Shut up!" screamed Ariadne. "I thought you'd been crushed by that cave in! I thought my big brother died!" She threw her arms around him and cried. Nathan looked down at her, and heard her wailing. It sent shivers down his spine to think how similar her cries sounded to his own a week ago when Ol' Chambo swallowed her whole. With seedlings of tears in his eyes, he gazed at Jessie and Paul, who wore expressions of concern and suspicion. Then he met Klein's gaze, which utterly perplexed him. It was only a brief look, but it seemed like Klein wanted to hit him harder than Ariadne.

It was gone in the next instant, and he slapped Nathan on his bare back.

"You'd better have a shower and get changed out of those muddy pants, eh?" he said with a grin.

* * *

Nathan was in and out of the shower in record time. He threw on a clean set of clothes as quickly as he could, taking a glance out the window at the falling sun. Astrid sat in his bed, wearing his pyjamas, with a perturbed and impatient expression.

"You should have just killed me," she growled in a whisper. "You could not have left your sister and friends in more danger."

"And I couldn't leave you in better hands," said Nathan flatly as he threw on his jacket. He brandished the paper with Chouno's home address, "I'll get the antidote as quickly as I can, and come back before that ugly mo-fo can take you."

"Big hero, eh?" grumbled a resigned Astrid.

"Don't have faith in me?" asked Nathan.

"Not in my ability to keep this thing at bay long enough,"

returned the girl. She tentatively wiggled her fingers, and cringed when her left pinky failed to respond. "The infection is advancing. I've got maybe three hours."

"I'll catch a fast bus then," said Nathan. He sat down next to her and silenced her. "You can't stop me. Right now, I'm going to do right what I tried to do a week ago. Because you did the same for me."

Astrid pursed her lips to swallow back her annoyed protest. She realised she was far too tired to argue with him. Instead, she said, "Just be safe, okay?"

Nathan grinned and started to feel bold, so he kissed her on the forehead. Her fist, though weak, embedded itself in his gut.

"Do that again, and I'll splatter your guts," she growled.

"Oi! I just thought the mood was nice," replied Nathan indignantly. "It's not like I groped your boobs or anything."

"Just get going, you bloody moron," snapped Astrid, though her red cheeks betrayed her anger as more shyness than violation.

Nathan stepped away and with a smirk he said, "Yes, Ma'am!"

"You end this, you hear me?" said Astrid with a militaristic tone reminiscent of a drill sergeant. "Find Chouno, stop him, and come back alive. Got it?"

Nathan punched his chest and said, "Got it."

He exited the room, and met with his friends in the common room. Ariadne approached him first and asked, "How's Astrid's back?"

"It's fine," replied Nathan. "But I need to go and get some meds for her. Can I get you guys to keep her company?"

"No problem. Just you don't fall down any hills, okay?" said Ariadne with an outstretched finger.

"Do you need one of us to come too?" asked Klein blandly. Again he had that same gaze in his eye that Nathan couldn't translate.

"I should be fine," he assured everyone. "Just keep

Astrid company and don't let her be alone tonight."

He said his byes and walked out of the dormitory building. He took it slow at first, to avoid his friends' suspicion. When he was out of view of the building, he broke into a sprint down the road.

* * *

Nathan's friends barged into the room, all at once. Astrid straightened herself up as the three boys and one girl plopped down on the bed or on chairs in the room. Ariadne started asking about Astrid and Nathan's common interest in paintball, which was a hard lie for Astrid to sell considering she'd never played the game. About half an hour or so went by, in which Astrid learned a little more about Nathan's friends.

As the redness of the sky started to darken, Jessie and Paul excused themselves to go finish some homework. Ariadne soon departed as well. That left Klein alone with the mysterious monster hunter, and a chance to finally sate his horrified curiosity.

"Plant people, huh?" he said as soon as Ariadne was out of the room. Astrid's eyes widened so much her eyeballs could have fallen from their sockets. She immediately flew into a splutter of coughing.

"How much did he tell you?" she asked eventually, with an air of heavy reluctance.

"*Nathan* told me jack all, except having a dream about getting killed trying to save a girl in a Catholic outfit," replied Klein, his arms tightly folded and his gaze stern and resolute. "Night before last, I followed you. I thought that Nathan might be doing the nasty with a girl other than you, which ain't cool. So I followed you, and I saw you with some weird Doc-Ock robot arms fight some half rose, half naked black chick monster thing. Needless to say, I haven't slept in two days, wondering what the fuck you've been doing with my best friend."

Astrid's gaze stooped downwards as he spoke, and she

silently cursed herself for her negligence in allowing more civilians to be dragged into her insane world. She didn't meet Klein's gaze as she mumbled, "Do they know?"

"I may be an idiot, but I'm not stupid," retorted Klein. "You know how much Ariadne'd be freaked out? Jessie and Paul are suspicious, but they don't know the half of it. And I don't want to tell them anything. I'm not even sure what I saw." He sat down next to her and forced her to look at him. "So, tell me what's going on?"

Astrid explained what had happened over the course of the week, leaving out as much about her agency as possible. Klein didn't say anything, and just listened stoically. He did, however, withdraw in disgust at the sight of the embryo, which had by then weaved its veiny, pulsating tentacles through and across her flesh.

"That's what Nathan's gone to get from Chouno," she said. "If he doesn't get back within three hours, I'm going to have to take my own life. Otherwise, I'll become a monster, like that woman, and kill everyone in this dorm."

Klein stood there a long time, his eyes fixed on Astrid and the thing in her belly, before he finally relaxed and said, "Typical Nathan."

"I beg your pardon?" asked Astrid, a little surprised that there was no screaming or mortified chiding.

"It's typical of Nathan to do that," he said with a resigned shrug. "He's almost obsessive, that guy. He just *has* to dive in to help people – even when they don't really need help." He pondered a moment as he sifted through his memories of his oldest friend. "Might have had something to do with that ball," he thought aloud.

"What ball?" asked Astrid, her curiosity piqued.

Klein leaned against the bed frame and recounted his story: "Way back when he and I were in, like, Year One … or Kindie, maybe… Anyway, he and I were playing cricket in his driveway. Ariadne was a little toddler and was walking around outside too. Nathan and I had put our pocket money together to buy one of those pro cricket balls. You know, the hard red ones they play pro matches with. Nathan bowls it, I knock it, and it goes right back at him. He ducks, it flies over him, and hits Ariadne on the head. This is a pro cricket ball, so pretty bloody heavy and hard. The girl needed like ten stitches and was in the hospital for a couple of days to make sure she didn't have brain damage. Luckily, her scar is above the hairline, so you can't see it. But I remember that look on Nathan's face when he saw her. It was like he'd killed her. And his parents yelled the shit out of him. Seriously, his name was dirt for weeks. But it really wasn't fair, you know. *I* was the one who hit it, and I tried to tell his parents. But they kept going off at him, telling him that 'He's the responsible one! Letting the ball hit his sister was as bad as throwing it at her himself!' What a crock of absolute horseshit, you know? And since then, he can't help himself. He's got the biggest messiah complex on the freaking planet."

Astrid covered her mouth in shock at the story, as so much of what perplexed her about Nathan started to gel in her head. The mismatched jigsaw pieces suddenly fell together.

"Now I understand why he seemed so interesting," she thought aloud. "I couldn't figure out why, when I first met him. He'd charged in and got himself killed without understanding the circumstances. I thought he was just a macho idiot trying to save the damsel. But then, even when he knew what he was getting himself into, after I explained everything to him, he still wanted to fight with me. Every time he'd gone the opposite of what I'd expected him to do, I thought he was just cocky, looking for attention, or trying to be cool."

"Well, if this Chouno kid is gonna do something bad to himself, you can probably guess what's going on in Nathan's head now," said Klein.

A horrible thought occurred to Astrid as she recalled what Nathan had told Burrumering before his decisive strike. A look of horror fell over her face.

"He'll die if he fights him alone," she whispered.

At that, Klein stepped forward and said, "Where is he headed?"

9 | Metamorphosis

The sun had dipped beneath the horizon before Nathan's taxi reached its destination. He took a quick glance around the cul-de-sac, which had only one exit through a Shinto-style arch. Through the darkness, a tiny point of light trickled down the long path to the gate, but it was so far away Nathan couldn't tell if it was a house or a street lamp. He paid his driver and waited for the car to drive away. The headlights disappeared, and all that remained was the moonlight seeping through the trees. Nathan made his way through the gate and up the path.

The place looked like something out of a Kurosawa movie. The sound of bamboo clattering punctuated every minute, typical of those garden water decorations. Nathan couldn't imagine going to sleep to that sound. Every minute would snap him back to the waking world.

Maybe that's what sent Chouno cuckoo, he wondered half-seriously.

There was a sudden click, a sound Nathan had only ever heard in movies, and his every hair stood on end. He subconsciously placed his hand to his heart, but kept his mouth shut. Out of the shadows stepped a man in a black suit, a gun cocked at his head.

"Stop right there, sir," said the man. "This is private property, and you're trespassing."

Nathan threw his hands in the air and quickly blurted, "I'm looking for the Koushaku family house. I'm a friend of Chouno."

The man cocked his head. The shadows concealed his pursed lips stifling his chuckles. He finally said, "I think you've got that backwards, mate. This is the Chouno family house."

I guess I got it wrong, thought Nathan in between alarmed pants. His gaze was still fixed on the gun aimed at him, and his brain frantically tried to convince itself that the Kakugane could heal a gunshot to the head.

"I'm Nathan Grant, I go to Warrawul Boarding School, and I'm a friend of Koushaku's," he blurted quickly. "The dorm roof caved in today and I just wanted to make sure he's okay."

The man paused a moment, then spoke into his collar, "Breach detected. Judged non-threatening. Just a schoolkid looking for the Young Master."

After a short exchange, in which the man confirmed Nathan's student ID, he holstered his weapon and beckoned Nathan to the house. It was exactly like in old samurai movies, complete with the rule that you have to lose your shoes before you step onto the landing. Nathan followed the guard, who slid aside one of the external canvas partitions and motioned for him to enter.

The Japanese man inside did not even look up from the desk over which he hunched, and merely muttered, "What do you want with Koushaku?"

Nathan assumed this man was Papillon's dad. He repeated his explanation regarding the caved-in roof of the dormitory. He left out anything to do with homunculi or Astrid.

Mister Chouno dropped his pen and growled furiously.

"Our house has been inundated with calls about Koushaku," he grumbled. Then he slapped the table and growled, "How many times will that stupid boy humiliate our family?"

"Stupid boy?" asked Nathan.

"I pour so much capital into that asset, and no return,"

barked Mister Chouno. "Reputable schooling, the best tutors money can buy, and then suddenly his grades fall, he quits school, and vandalizes his dormitory! Foolish, useless child!"

Nathan's neck muscles tightened and he blurted, "He didn't vandalize anything!"

Not quite true, he thought.

"Hey, didn't you know he was sick?" he quickly asked.

Mister Chouno shot Nathan a mortified look, as if he'd just been accused of the most vulgar crime possible. He murmured in a low growl, "How did you know that? Who told you?"

"Your son did," replied Nathan as if it were the most obvious thing in the universe.

That only made Mister Chouno even angrier, and he upturned his desk in a fit of fury.

"How dare that fool shame our name so?" he snarled. "He was sworn to secrecy. After all I've done for that child, he exposes us to ridicule!"

Nathan's head filled with a cocktail of bewilderment and distain. He opened his mouth, intent on rebuking the old man, but was so taken aback by the sheer insanity that he couldn't think of anything to say.

If my son was dying, I wouldn't be going tropo at someone whose just tryin' to help, he thought.

"Your son was dying and you keep it a secret?" he stammered.

"You act as if there was no treatment! There was treatment, but it didn't work," retorted Mister Chouno.

"That's no excuse to keep it a secret!" barked Nathan, who had finally found his words.

Mister Chouno poked the air dangerously close to Nathan's nose, and he growled, "What happens in *my* family is *none* of your business!"

"Whatever, you old fart," retorted Nathan. "I'd like to talk to him."

Mister Chouno's expression turned into rage-tainted

bewilderment.

"He isn't here," he snapped. "I don't know where he is. Could not possibly care less."

Nathan again lost his breath, and for a moment considered that the man was joking. He looked around to the guards, who wore blank, serious faces. Then he saw another face through the door to the adjacent room, a spitting image of his quarry.

"Chouno!" he barked as he charged toward the boy. In the next instant, he was on the tatami floor, held there by two other guards.

"Who is this rambling idiot, Father?" uttered the boy, though his tone of voice was slightly different from the Chouno Nathan knew. For one, it was much less sickly.

"He's looking for Koushaku," replied the out-of-breath father. To Nathan, he barked, "He is not here, and hasn't been here for years. Take your business elsewhere." He motioned to the guards to kick the boy out. As Nathan was dragged away, he heard the old man bellow, "If you find him, tell him that he's officially cut-off. His younger brother, Jiro, will be the new heir to Chouno Industries."

Nathan grazed his face against the asphalt, and looked up to see the guards standing as a barricade around the gate to the Chouno estate. One of them even made the clichéd gesture of dusting his hands off. They kept their eyes fixed on him as he pulled himself to his feet and trudged away.

No way that's a real dad, thought Nathan. *Papillon's gotta be in there, just hiding.*

Chouno's face came to mind. He recalled the boy sitting in the dorm room, and the expression he wore as he sat there, doubled over in pain. Nathan wondered if that was the expression all people wore at the end of their rope. Then he recalled the sheer anger in the father's eyes when Nathan said he knew about the illness, and pondered whether it was more shame for his son, or for himself.

No, if I were Chouno, I'd not come back here for anything, he concluded. *So, if I had an incurable illness, and didn't have a home to go back to, where would I be?*

Nathan chewed the tip of his thumb as he walked away from the cul-de-sac and reached the main road. He took a moment to lament letting the taxi go. That then led his thought train to what he saw on the way over. An image filled his mind: a block of warehouses with a butterfly logo, the very same as the watermark on the documents on the father's desk.

Nathan suddenly broke into a sprint down the road. He took a few turns until he found the gate with the butterfly logo. After gauging the fence, he concluded he wouldn't be able to jump over it, and decided to look around for another access point. He saw something in the dim moonlight, and after shining his phone torch over it, he recognised a pair of pliers discarded in the grass. Nearby was a hole in the wireframe fencing, just large enough for a boy of Chouno's size to crawl through.

He earned himself a few painful scratches as he struggled through the razor sharp barrier, and when he was through he sprinted down the path lined by warehouses. He scanned the area, looking for any semblance of light that would betray habitation.

Where the hell are you, Chouno?

He checked his watch and saw the second hand tick the minutes away. It almost mocked him, as it seemed to skip notches on its way to the twelve-marker. His cracked ribs ached, and his legs waned in their already diminished strength. His frustration built to breaking point and he looked into the night sky.

"Oi! Chouno! Get your arse out here, now!" he roared. As the echoes came back to him, so did another sound. It sounded like something dropping to the floor, and he grabbed onto it like it was the last lifeline in a landslide. He sprinted toward the sound, and saw a faint red light patter its way out of a window of one of the warehouses. He gave a hefty yawp as he threw his weight against the door of the building.

Two minutes later, he gingerly opened the door while wincing at a sprained shoulder.

Chouno stood up, his face a confused mess of annoyance and alarm. A used futon was laid on the floor, surrounded by empty pill-bottles and noodle cups. Near it was the source of the red light: a compact machine that resembled a high-tech 3D printer. Instead of printing something, the device's tubes and conduits led into the pear-shaped vial with the near-maturity homunculus embryo within. It vibrated with red luminance that feebly filled the room.

"I see Burrumering failed," mumbled Chouno.

"He died well, a hell of a lot better than your toad," replied Nathan.

"He didn't fulfil my orders, so he was just as useless as the rest," Chouno growled, though his eyes were so blank Nathan thought he was high.

Nathan advanced, slowly uttering, "I promised him that I wouldn't kill you. And I plan to keep that promise. Give me the antidote and that embryo."

Chouno pointed to a safe in the corner.

"The antidote is in there," said the sickly boy. "I'll give you the key and you can go, but you're not taking my new life!"

Nathan let go of his sore shoulder with a grimace. With his eyes focused on the pulsating embryo in the vial, he said, "It won't be much of a life, Chouno. You're a murderer in this life. And you'll be one in your new life. Even if I fail, and Astrid dies, someone else from her agency will come after you, and you'll die anyway."

"The bastards'll have one hell of a fight on their hands," retorted Chouno as he edged nearer to the incubator. "I told you, I don't care who I have to kill to live. And there's no reason I can't create more homunculi to be my slaves. Your girlfriend will be the first, and when she turns, I'll have her Kakugane and be invincible!" He doubled over as his fervour exacerbated his illness. Blood gushed through the fingers of the hand with which he covered his mouth. Nathan just shook his head, his eyes radiating his own sorrow for the poor boy.

"You'll die alone," he lamented.

"Wow! You make it sound like that wasn't going to happen no matter what I did," growled Chouno, tears near his eyes.

"It won't if you stop," said Nathan, his gaze unwavering as he moved closer to the boy. "I'll be there with you in the end, I swear it."

Chouno paused a moment, his breath caught in his throat, as if he were considering the act of charity. In the next instant, he grinned sardonically, "Pass!"

"Of course, he'd pass," exclaimed a voice from outside the warehouse. Nathan recognised it before he turned to see Jiro, leaning against the doorframe. He looked through Nathan and bore a hole into his older brother's head. "It wouldn't matter if the most famous and beloved person in the world offered vigil at your bedside, anyone would rather not die."

Nathan's gaze darted between the two brothers as he tried to figure out what to do. Before he could open his mouth, four of the house guards appeared and restrained him and Chouno. Jiro lifted Nathan's head by his hair and studied him as he would a catfish he'd just caught. Nathan's eyes widened at Jiro's features.

"It's like you're a Chouno clone," he mumbled. A fist suddenly struck his face like a meteorite, and blood trickled from a loosened tooth.

"Do not call me a clone," growled Jiro. "I've had enough with my useless brother being a basis for comparison."

Chouno sneered at his younger brother, and asked, "What do you want, Jiro?"

Jiro suddenly kneed Nathan in the gut and shrieked, "You didn't tell him! Useless bloody messenger!" He composed himself and turned to his older brother. "You've been cut-off, officially. Father has made me successor to the family."

"Boring," retorted Chouno with as much sarcasm as his weakening body would allow. "Enjoy your throne, Jiro. I don't care anymore."

"Oh, but *I* care," said Jiro as he drew near. "It's all I've ever cared about … Making Mother and Father happy. But even when I slaved for their approval, they only ever focused on you. And when Mother died, I begged for Father's consolation, but he only focused on you and made sure *you* were happy. It was always about you … bloody *you!*" He gripped his brother's neck, and dug his nails into the skin as hard as he could. Blood started to trickle from the wounds as Jiro savagely growled, "I was nothing. Mother and Father had their star child, and I was, what? Leftovers? A spare? Just because you were born ten minutes earlier, you got to have the honour of bearing the *shaku* suffix of our great grandfather! You had all the prestige; I had nothing. *Nothing!*"

Jiro released his brother's neck with a shove and waltzed over to the incubator. Nathan gagged as he watched Jiro lick the blood from his fingers while studying the machine.

"I didn't really understand what you two were talking about earlier, but I assume this is some chicanery to cure you of your illness?" Jiro asked, an air of genuine curiosity in his voice.

"Stay away from it," snapped Chouno, that familiar psychotic rage radiating from his eyes.

Jiro pressed his fingers to his lips like a comic relief in an old cartoon, and edged his heel toward the pear-shaped vial.

"Wouldn't it be sad if someone knocked this over?" he said in a squeaky, effeminate voice.

"Don't do it! *Yamerou, kusoyarou!*" Chouno screeched. The anguish in his voice only goaded Jiro's sadism, and he kicked the incubator like a soccer ball. The device disintegrated under the force of his foot, and the wailing contents of the shattered vial flew against the wall. Chouno's dismayed shriek was overshadowed only by Jiro's victorious laughter. The younger brother danced on one foot, giggling and shrieking with glee. He then charged at his brother and proceeded to punch and kick the mortified boy.

"Die! You useless shit! Just die!" he screeched over and over, as he threw punch after agonising punch into his brother's face. Nathan struggled desperately against the vice-grip of the two guards, and pleaded with them to stop, but his voice was drowned out by the yawps of the younger brother. The boy finally ran out of stamina and backed away to admire his work.

Chouno crumpled to the ground, barely a flicker of life left in him. Blood gushed from his mouth and nose, which formed a gory puddle around him. A tiny sliver of strength remained, and he used it to look at the drop of goo, flitting about in a puddle of synthetic amniotic fluid and glass shards. Suddenly, he launched into a desperate crawl, his tongue hanging from his bruised face as he charged like a wild dog toward the embryo.

"Stop!" screamed Nathan.

Chouno slid the rest of the way, until his forehead touched the embryo. In an instant, the thing launched into his skin, and dug through the flesh and bone until it was gone all the way inside him. Chouno fell limp a moment. Then his legs and arms began to twitch, like electric shocks were flowing through his dead limbs. Then his whole body contorted and shuddered, and he let out a gut-wrenching scream.

Jiro and the guards watched in confusion, while Nathan gazed in sheer terror. At first, it seemed like Chouno's soiled uniform was shrinking, until everyone blinked a few times and realised *he* had grown. The uniform ripped at the seams until all that remained was a pair of tight undies with, bizarrely, a butterfly pattern. Finally, the body finished writhing, and lay still.

Then his eyes opened, radiating a deep green hue.

The lean, muscular entity rose to its full height – almost

two metres – and turned to Jiro. The boy cowered silently, too terrified of the being before him to run or even scream. The thing's pristine pale skin glistened in the moonlight as he lifted Jiro by the neck and murmured, "Grant ... you didn't want me to become a *choujin*? Too bad."

"No!" cried Nathan.

The beast's jaw dislocated and its mouth widened to a sickening maw. Jiro's shriek was cut off in a sickening gurgle as the monster's teeth dove into his neck. His flesh cascaded into the monster's mouth, until all that remained was his skeleton, stripped clean. As the bones of his victim clattered to the ground, the beast burped and let out a satisfied moan.

"Hot as hell, and sweet as a kiss," he chuckled. "Ah! This is the taste of human meat!" The monster's deep green eyes turned to the two guards nearest to Jiro's remains. Before they could even think to reach for their guns, the thing pounced upon the nearest wailing man. In an instant, his flesh vanished with the voracious slurping sounds of a two-year-old devouring spaghetti. With a wet gurgle, the creature latched onto the other man's head and glugged his flesh away.

The beast threw its head backward with a wide, blood-soaked grin and laughed hysterically.

"This is my power! This is my strength! Ah, my new life!"

Nathan was mortified at his failure. The guards holding him were horrified by the sight, and fumbled to draw their guns.

The beast reached into his torn and discarded uniform, and drew a butterfly mask, which went straight onto his face. With a gleeful smile, the beast proclaimed, "My transformation is complete! Koushaku Chouno is dead. You can call me Papillon!" He sung the name with utter gusto as he pirouetted about the warehouse.

The terrified guards finally worked the safety off their guns and unleashed a flurry of bullets at Papillon. All he did was pose like the world's most famous and beloved underwear model, as the bullets deflected harmlessly off his skin. The guns clicked empty. The guards' blood ran cold as Papillon approached them, dwarfing them by size. He swiftly ripped an arm off one guard and bludgeoned the other with it. He devoured them both, but not fast enough for at least one of them to scream, "Monster!"

Papillon drew deep of the scent of blood and roared, "I am no monster! I am a *choujin!*"

He panted as his body flooded with ecstasy, which was only augmented by the meaty aftertaste that lingered in his throat. He heard someone fall over behind him, and turned to see Nathan, his eyes full of fearful and remorseful tears.

"Whacha think, Grant?" asked the blood-stained creature. He struck an elegant pose. "Am I not too sexy for a shirt?"

"What happened to not eating humans?" was all the flabbergasted boy could ask.

"I lied," giggled Papillon.

Nathan gritted his teeth, pushed away his fear and sorrow, and launched to his feet. He raised his hands to his chest, but could not even utter a syllable before Papillon ran him through with his long, sharp, green nails. Nathan collapsed as Papillon licked the blood from his fingers. The homunculus hefted the wounded boy into the air and moved to consume him.

He hesitated.

"That girl will be a homunculus before long," he intoned. When Nathan only grimaced in reply, Papillon continued, "She is dear to you, isn't she? The woman who saved your life; who gave you new life." He pondered a little longer, then jovially blurted, "I'll hold off on eating you then!"

Papillon threw Nathan into the asphalt, shattering the ground beneath.

"We'll wait for her to become my slave," he said as he leaned down to the fallen heap on the ground. "I'll make her kill your friends, and eat that delectable little sister of yours.

I'll make you watch as it happens. Then you'll watch as your school … No, your town! No! The world! You'll watch it all burn beneath my heel. And when you've realised how meaningless your whole plight was, I'll devour you, one cell at a time!"

Papillon said so much, so fervently, within a single breath that he almost passed out. He straightened up, a little bewildered at his fatigue, and shook his head to clear it.

"My, my! This body uses a lot of energy," he thought aloud. "Perhaps I'll feed a little more."

His eyes drifted to the bright lights of the Chouno Estate, and his lips cracked sinisterly. "Bon Appétit!"

10 | Papillon

A fugue of dull discomfort enveloped the lingering fragments of Nathan's consciousness. A cacophony of pops and faint tortured screams wafted away the haze, and drew him into the waking world. Every nerve in his body fizzled with pain. He tried to push himself up from the asphalt, but his elbows and shoulders buckled and he fell back down onto the ground.

He could still hear the screaming men and their sudden strangled gurgles amid the distant bangs of their futile gunfire. His mind could not help itself, and conjured up visions to accompany the hellish din: torn flesh spewing forth a red metallic-tasting haze, countless families mourning a pile of corpses. His parents' voices echoed in his mind's ear, "You let this happen! It's as bad as if you killed them yourself!"

The insides of his brain seemed to fill with hot flaming liquid, and it singed his every nerve. He tried to shut the voices out, but they came back even harder and propounded the vision of his sister, disappearing behind the snake's teeth, into his head. And those voices repeated, "You let this happen!"

"No, I didn't," Nathan roared aloud, and pounded his hand into the ground. Amazingly, he felt no pain. At first, he thought he was already in so much pain that his brain didn't care about new injuries. Then he looked up, and saw a hefty crack in the asphalt where his hand had struck it. There was not a scratch on his knuckles. As he gazed at his hand, mesmerised by what he saw, he heard Astrid's far more pleasant voice: *Kakugane resonates with the soul and gives form to our will to live. When you are about to lose that which you live for, use it!*

Those words, which seemed as if they'd been spoken in another eon, filled him with strength. He pressed his palms to the ground and pushed. He gained enough height on his shuddering arms to put his foot down, and then his other one. Finally, he'd reached his feet. Despite his shuddering body, he forced himself to stand tall. Steadying his breathing, he pushed his thoughts to Ariadne as she was now: a happy Year Seven kid, playing with her friends. After that, his thoughts more easily drifted to Klein, Jessie, and Paul, playing *Smash Brothers* on the TV with him. Then he saw Astrid, in her plain clothes. She smiled at him, and moved to kiss him.

"Mate, not the time for naughty fantasies," he self-chided.

Nathan looked down at the rest of his body. The pain had dimmed enough for him to move more comfortably, and he started to walk toward the gate. He crawled through the hole in the wire fence, and paced steadily back to the Chouno house. The screams subsided just as he got there. At the main gate, he saw stripped skeletons scattered about. Further inwards, he could see blood splattered across the Japanese-style partitions. Clothes and bones carpeted the landing and the tatami mats inside. Nathan found the office where Mister Chouno had been working, and saw only bones and the robes the man had worn, torn and bloodied.

The house suddenly shuddered with the sound of wood and fibro shattering. Nathan scrambled out of the house as quickly as he could, and looked up to see Papillon, still in his undies, and even more dried entrails covering his face. He laughed hysterically, like a clichéd super-villain ready to take over the world.

"Let the new world of Papillon begin with the burning of the old!" he bellowed.

"Papillon!" Nathan cried.

The homunculus looked down, his grin not wavering but widening, and he snapped, "What?"

Nathan defiantly placed his hand to his heart and roared, "Arms Alchemy!"

Papillon advanced on the boy, but didn't expect the flash of light from Nathan's chest. He winced at the light, and hit the ground with a thud. His eyes cleared just in time to see Nathan's spear coming at him and he dodged it. Papillon launched to his feet and charged at the lancer, swiping and slashing, but finding his accuracy much lower than before. Nathan parried his bare-handed blows, and dodged the ones he couldn't. He pulled back as the much taller Papillon drew closer, trying to gain as much ground as he could.

Papillon's fury and frustration grew as his strikes repeatedly failed to find the smaller boy. Nathan deflected one blow and moved to counter with the tip of his spear. Papillon darted to the side, allowed the spear to pass, and let Nathan's body follow it directly into his hand. Caught by the scruff of the neck, Nathan started to fill with panic in anticipation of that voracious maw he'd seen in action one too many times.

For some reason, though, Papillon still didn't eat him.

Instead, the outraged homunculus threw him toward the house. He flew through several partitions and walls, until he came to rest in a garden in the middle of the house. Blood from his wounds tainted the garden ponds and smattered the plants with dirty red droplets. He frantically pulled himself out of the plants and looked around for his spear, which lay on the landing nearby. He didn't have a chance to grab it before a long-nailed, immensely strong hand grabbed his neck. Papillon glared at him from behind his butterfly mask.

"Useless fool," he growled. "You should have just laid there in despair. Now I'm gonna have to hurt you even more!" He threw Nathan down onto the damp garden ground and held his throat tightly. "Why bother coming here, Grant? I've already devoured everyone. Jiro, Father, his servants and guards, all of them! They're all in my gut!"

"They were your family," Nathan breathily growled.

"No, they weren't," retorted Papillon. "At first I thought I'd spare anyone who could tell me apart from Jiro, but no one could. Tough luck for them, but it did tell me something: Koushaku Chouno didn't die tonight, but long ago. That past is as meaningless to me now as this house. That family, that school, that life! It's all gone now. All that remains is I, Papillon!"

A voice reached Nathan's ears that both mortified and thrilled him. It said, "And ya got no one to help ya now!"

Papillon released Nathan's throat and turned around. In the next instant, his body from the neck down was as a lump of string tied to the ball that was his head, flying helplessly across the landing and into the wall. Nathan looked up from the ground and saw Klein with a hardwood cricket bat in his hands.

"Howzat, motherfucker!" he roared. He threw his forefingers in the air and swivelled to marvel at his awesomeness.

"What the hell're you doing here?" yelled Nathan

As Klein helped Nathan to his feet, he pointed to one of the house's support columns, against which Astrid sat, still in pyjamas and deathly pale. Nathan could see the tentacles from the embryo drawing nearer to the base of her skull.

"I saw her fighting one of these things the other night, and knew you'd gotten in deep with something," said Klein. "I got her to explain everything, and we came over to help."

Papillon rose to his feet, sporting a big purple bruise across his cheek. In her daze, Astrid looked over at the homunculus, and couldn't help but raise her eyebrows in confusion and surprise.

Something's wrong, she thought.

Papillon was too filled with rage to notice her and

charged at Klein, bellowing, "What good can a sports jock do?"

Nathan shoved Klein out of the way and darted backward, so that Papillon narrowly missed them both. He leapt toward his spear, and swiped it to ward Papillon off. The beast was far too furious to be held at bay. With a manic pirouette, he kicked Nathan aside and charged Klein. The boy didn't have the element of surprise anymore, and his earlier cockiness evaporated as he beheld the fury of the beast. Instinctively, he held the bat out to block Papillon's swipe of pure rage, but it disintegrated under the sheer force of the blow, which sent him through the wall.

"I'll kill that little maggot and eat him," Papillon growled. Nathan put himself between the creature and his quarry, his spear pointed at Papillon's head.

"No more deaths," he said sternly.

"Or what? You'll kill me?" the beast taunted. He moved to stab his enemy, who blocked it with his lance. At that moment, Astrid announced her presence to the beast as she yelled, "Nathan! Take this!"

A hexagonal talisman flew from the girl into Nathan's hand. He and Papillon looked at it a moment, before Nathan's mouth widened into a toothy grin.

"Double Arms Alchemy!" he roared.

A second lance materialised in his hand, bearing a similar colour scheme to Astrid's robotic arms. She grinned excitedly as Nathan swiped and lunged against the beast. Papillon started to lose ground, slipping on the wet garden soil as he faltered under Nathan's twin-spear attacks. Nathan put his foot into Papillon's stomach and he flew backward, doubled over in pain.

"Nathan, hold it!" cried Astrid. She panted a moment, in as much pain as Papillon, who subsequently let out a bloody retch. The familiar sound of his vomiting gave her an epiphany.

"The embryo wasn't complete, was it?" she asked both of them.

"His younger brother destroyed the incubator, but he was desperate and used the thing anyway," replied Nathan.

Astrid started to cough, then giggle, before laughing with about as much gusto as Papillon had earlier.

"Your transformation into Papillon was a complete failure," she snarled. "You used an immature embryo, and instead of curing you, it turned your sickly body itself into a homunculus." Papillon glared at Astrid, whose grin screamed poetic justice. "You murdered so many innocent people to escape your disease, and in the end you just imprisoned yourself in a life of nothing but your disease! You're going to *live* in excruciating pain, and now you know *why!*"

Papillon gave a frustrated, pain-ridden wail as the truth fell upon his ears like a funerary gong. His glare darted between Nathan and Astrid, and when he saw the tendrils snaking toward her skull, his expression turned into his signature grin. He rose to his full height, slipped his hands into his undies and procured a key.

"Remember that safe?" he intoned. Nathan gasped as the key disappeared down Papillon's throat. Then Papillon opened his arms, wide and accepting, and proclaimed, "Come and get me!"

Nathan pointed his spears forward and charged. When he struck Papillon's palms, they stopped him dead in his tracks. He pressed forward, but Papillon wouldn't budge. It was as if a brick wall stood between him and the monster.

The monster roared, "I'll eat you, take those Kakugane, and use them to make another new life! And you cannot stop me!"

Ariadne, Klein, Jessie, Paul, Ol' Chambo, Burrumering, Astrid. Their faces flashed through Nathan's memory, and before he knew it, they'd filled him with strength. He suddenly burst through that impenetrable wall, and took Papillon with him.

The dust and smoke cleared. Papillon hung, crucified between two wooden pillars in the ruins of the Chouno house, the lances holding him in place. The *choujin* dangled there unceremoniously, sneering at his slayer, who only returned his cursing stare with a pitying glare of his own.

"Now what?" he grumbled. "You've beaten me. But if you don't get that antidote soon, she'll be a monster. You said 'No more deaths,' so will you wait to sift through my excrement?"

A single tear dribbled from Nathan's eye and, holding his gaze, he said, "I'm sorry, mate."

At that, Papillon's eyes widened in surprise, and for once he actually looked Nathan in the eye. He saw the tear, the reluctance, and the resignation. Completely taken aback, his brain simply refused to process what he saw and what he felt. Suddenly, one of the spears was plunged into his stomach, and his lower half disintegrated. If there was pain, Papillon was too befuddled and flabbergasted to process it. He saw Nathan bend down to pick up the key from within the vaporising mass, and the boy sorrowfully murmured, "I'm so sorry, Koushaku Chouno!"

At that, his usual acerbic personality came to full dominance. With a grin that could only be described as Chouno-esque, he snapped, "Don't apologise to me, you hypocrite!"

The other spear slashed through his torso, along with the two columns that held him up. The roof collapsed in a thunderous crash, and Papillon was gone.

Nathan sniffed back his last tear, returned the spears to their inert form, and raced back to Astrid with the key.

"Sorry, I know how you feel about being carried," he said before scooping her up into his arms. She was unresponsive, save for a few subtle gurgles to show she was still alive.

"Oi, Klein, you alright?" Nathan bellowed. Some ruffling in the debris signalled Klein's awakening. He emerged with a stream of blood flowing from his forehead, and he looked dizzy. When he saw Nathan with an unconscious Astrid in his arms, he snapped straight to attention.

"You got the antidote?" he asked with a slight slur. Nathan brandished the key and beckoned his friend to follow.

Outside the house was Klein's car, its engine still running. Under Nathan's direction, Klein peeled out of the gate, and the car almost tumbled as it turned onto the main road. Klein stamped his feet on the gas and burst through the gates of the warehouse complex toward Chouno's hideout.

The safe was there, in the corner, just where Chouno left it. Klein fumbled with the lock while Nathan held Astrid. He saw the tentacles approaching her hairline, and his own heart thumped with fear.

"Come on, goddamn it," he screamed. The safe swung open and Klein tossed the syringe through the air toward him. He caught it in his shaking hand, bit off the lid, and jammed the needle into the embryo.

11 | The Starlight Lancer

A bright yellow light stung at Nathan's closed eyelids and roused him from a restless slumber. A combination of the previous night's adventures and the uncomfortable hotel chair on which he'd curled up had helped to keep him awake. But what really did the trick was the girl over whom he maintained a concerned vigil.

After he and Klein had brought Astrid back to her hotel room, he sent his friend home, and then watched her until he could no longer hold back his drowsiness. His hand, pressed against his chest, twitched with every unconscious moan that left her lips.

Having realised he'd drifted off, Nathan shot to his feet. Astrid was up, standing in front of the mirror, gazing at her stomach as she ran her hands over it. He called out to her, and she turned to him and smiled.

"It's gone," she mumbled. "The pain is gone!"

Nathan grinned ecstatically and threw his arms around her. They both laughed victoriously and twirled around in the embrace. Nathan sobered a little and looked into her eyes. They were sparkling with gratitude. That typically-him boldness crept into his mind and he edged his hand up to her cheek.

"Forget it," she said curtly.

His boldness vanished, and frustration and disappointment rushed in to replace it.

"Oh, come on," he cried. "I was so cool! I got the

antidote and saved your life. The least you could do is give me a peck on the cheek."

Astrid rolled her eyes and grabbed his shoulder to stop his irate pacing.

"I will buy you breakfast," she said.

Nathan pouted, his arms crossed, and made a show of petulant defiance, before he finally said, "Pancakes."

Two showers, a brief walk, and a half-hour wait later, they sat in a coffee shop near Astrid's hotel. A three stack with maple syrup landed in front of each of them. They hoed into the meal like soldiers enjoying a victory feast. Nathan took a moment from enjoying the sugary goodness to grab a newspaper from the stand nearby. On the front cover it read, "Billionaire Family Decimated!"

Astrid noticed it as well, and Nathan started to read the story aloud, "Last night, the house of Shishaku Chouno, C.E.O. of Chouno Industries, was savagely attacked. The C.E.O., his son Jiro, and their staff were killed in a grizzly fashion, their bones seemingly stripped of their flesh. While authorities are investigating, a lone survivor has recounted her tale. 'I was preparing the bedding for the master, when I heard gunshots. I saw, out the window, the ghost of Koushaku, the eldest son who had died. He devoured everyone, pulled the muscles and organs right off their bones. It was horrible!'"

Nathan couldn't read further, and slapped the newspaper on the table. He edged his hand toward the fork, but his appetite was gone as the sounds and sights of the previous night came to mind. Astrid eyed him, and pursed her lips remorsefully. She looked like she was searching for any words to console him, but came up empty. Her mind went to the survivor's tale, and her mind immediately filled with concern that the woman had witnessed their battle. She grabbed the newspaper and read the rest of the article.

She grinned.

"What?" asked Nathan when he saw her smile.

Astrid cleared her throat and read on, "This story seems

like something from a epic fairy tale. The witness continues, 'I tried to hide, so that the ghost of the young master would not see me. Then I saw a boy appear to confront the demon, with a lance made of starlight. He did battle with the demon, defeated it, and the young master was at peace. This boy must have known the young master, and loved him dearly.'" She gazed at Nathan, who wore a pensive expression. She perused the remainder in silence, before landing on a paragraph that made her eyes bug out in shock. "Oh, this is not good."

Nathan grabbed the newspaper and read on from where Astrid indicated, "While it seems this story is outside the realm of reality, security footage was found from within the Chouno house that may corroborate her story. Much of the data was reported lost by investigators, but a few images have been recovered."

Above the columns were pixelated monochrome images of the Chouno house. Luckily, Nathan's face was unrecognisable, but the shining lance was unmistakable. Nathan and Astrid exchanged amazed but nervous glances. What followed in the article assuaged their concern a little.

"Authorities have not been able to identify the individual in the images. The police are calling for this 'Starlight Lancer' to submit himself or herself for questioning."

Nathan leaned back in his chair, a bit more relieved.

I don't have to do a thing, he thought. *Just keep quiet, and the cop's'll stop asking questions.*

His mind went to the survivor's account, and how she described Papillon's final moments.

"She said he was at peace," he mumbled. He picked up his fork and swallowed another mouthful of syrup-soaked pancake. "I suppose I can live with that."

Astrid smiled warmly and said, "You did really well, Nathan."

"Oh, and that name! *Starlight Lancer!*" he exclaimed, his eyes glossing over with excitement. "Now that is a kickass superhero name. Maybe that can be the name for my Arms

Alchemy."

Astrid pursed her lips, half of which upturned into a smile as she pondered a moment. Then she blurted, "Nah!"

"Oh, come on, it'd be awesome! I'll be the Starlight Lancer, and you can be the Spartan Valkyrie," retorted Nathan.

"Not happening," she retorted. "Besides, 'Starlight Lancer' doesn't work as a name for the weapon. You know what? When the sash lights up, it looks like a sunrise. How about 'Sunlight's Heart?'"

Nathan grinned excitedly as a comic book cover appeared in his head, entitled 'Starlight Lancer and his Amazing Sunlight Heart.' He chuckled giddily, "I love it."

They finished their breakfast and headed back to the hotel. Nathan's mind wandered to all the superhero adventures the Starlight Lancer would embark upon. They stopped out the front of the hotel, and faced each other.

"Well then, I'm a little late for school, but that's fine," said Nathan. "Talk later?"

Astrid shook her head and sighed.

"No," she said. "I have to report to my agency. Someone should come around to debrief you, but they should let you keep this." She pointed to his chest. "So long as you don't use it."

Nathan grimaced.

"You're coming back, though, right?" he asked hopefully.

"Maybe," murmured Astrid, shaking her head.

Nathan shifted his weight back and forth on his heels as he searched for something to say. Astrid moved near to him, and he thought he was finally going to get that kiss he'd been vectoring for. Instead, she held up her clenched fist. Nathan looked at it with a dopey expression, before her intent dawned on him, and he took the fist-bump as a befitting consolation.

Astrid nodded him toward the bus stop. He reluctantly turned and headed toward the bus that had just pulled up.

Nervously, Nathan looked over his shoulder to Astrid, but she was gone. A twinge of disappointment flooded through him. He tried to shrug it off, but couldn't shake the bittersweetness of their parting.

Nathan sighed, and hopped onto a bus headed for his dormitory. Everyone else was at school already, so the building was mostly empty. As he headed for his room, he saw a notice of change of management on the announcement board, and hummed with half-piqued interest.

Maybe the guy got sick of all the crazy stuff happening around here, he thought. *Hopefully the next one won't be a complete tight-arse.*

He changed into his uniform, grabbed his bag, and trotted off to school. He arrived just as the bell was ringing, and got to his locker just as the crowd of students started to disperse.

The whole area fell silent as he opened his locker. At first, he paid it no mind, but he soon realised every student was looking at him. He gazed around, and saw a collage of eyes shining lasers of curiosity at him. He went through the usual checks, such as making sure he was wearing pants – he was – and that his locker didn't have any contraband or embarrassing contents – it didn't.

Before he could ask what was the matter, Jessie and Paul appeared near him. Over their shoulders, he saw Klein, his face buried in his palms. Ariadne stood next to him, with an expression not unlike that of a child on Christmas morning.

"Nathan, can we ask you something?" Jessie stammered.

"Sure," said Nathan, quite perturbed at the scene.

Paul then curtly asked, "Are you the Starlight Lancer?"

Epilogue

A slender woman, wearing a black dress and cream-coloured blazer, climbed the stairs of the fire exit. Reaching the top floor, she flipped her blonde hair from her face and pushed to open the door. It wouldn't budge.

"Frick," she cursed, before clenching her fist. Her fist erupted with bright white light, and she swung it at the exit. The door swung open, deformed and almost torn from its hinges. Her fist returned to normal and she relaxed it, adjusting the eye-patch on her otherwise spotless face. She then marched onto the roof.

The night was chilly, and quite windy to boot. This was the first time she'd been back to Tokyo in a long while, and she was keen to get indoors as soon as she'd found what she was looking for.

She stopped at the edge of the roof, looked toward Tokyo Tower, and saw it. With a chuckle, she took a phone from her pocket, a cartoon skull emblazoned on its back cover, and dialled. As the call connected, she kept her gaze fixed on what she saw at the top of the building: a little girl with short chestnut hair, in a custom-made costume, a winged plush toy floating beside her, and a pink bird-head staff in her hand.

"Spirit, it's Marie," she said with a grin. "Inform Lord Reaper. They've awakened."

About the Author

Craig Stephen Cooper grew up in Wollongong, New South Wales, Australia. At a young age, he quickly developed a flare for the dramatic, an obsession with various video games, and an aptitude for expressiveness.

In response to his desire to develop video games, his parents allowed him to study software engineering under a tutor while still in primary school. At the same time, he took dance lessons after school. He later decided drama was a path better suited to his love of storytelling, and studied speech and drama during high school.

While completing a Bachelor of Computer Engineering, he underwent practical and theory examinations for an Associate Diploma of Performance Art. During his Doctor of Philosophy in Telecommunications, he taught speech and drama to primary school children. As a member of the Fellowship of Australian Writers, he has presented workshops on storytelling and poetry, drawing on his speech and drama studies.

Cooper conceived of *The AXOM* Saga while on a train from Fukuoka to Nagasaki in Japan. Under encouragement from his friends, he wrote the stories with a passion to equal his first novel, *Final Flight of the Ranegr*.

He also dabbles in video game and mobile app development.

About the Illustrator

Tessa Eden grew up upon the shores of Australia's sunny beaches, frolicking in the sand and exploring the beautiful underwater world. Her father being a software engineer, and mother an illustrator, it was natural that she would grow to combine the two, becoming a digital artist. She now spends her days painting digitally, and creating 3D animations and CGI for animation studios in Sydney.